"You've never told even a little white lie?"

Adam asked.

"Of course I have. I'm only human." Never before had Mandy felt so human—this man made her feel like a melting marshmallow over a hot fire.

He pulled her close, until her breasts grazed his chest. The steam from the wallpapering they'd been doing gave her skin a dewy sheen and he wanted to show her just how human he found her. He wanted to kiss her until she couldn't think, couldn't speak. Until he'd tasted those soft lips and she'd had a taste of what he had to offer—

But he wasn't there to kiss his best friend's prospective fiancée. It would be wrong....

Dear Reader,

Silhouette Romance rings in the New Year with a great new FABULOUS FATHER from bestselling author Elizabeth August! Murdock Parnell may be the *Ideal Dad* for eight-year-old Jeremy Galvin, but will he convince Jeremy's pretty mom, Irene, that he's her ideal husband?

In Kristin Morgan's latest book, Brianna Stansbury is *A Bride To Be*. Problem is, her groom-to-be is up to no good. It's up to Drew Naquin to rescue Brianna—even if that means marrying her himself!

Expectant Bachelor concludes Sandra Steffen's heartwarming WEDDING WAGER series about three brothers who vow they'll never say "I do." This time, Taylor Harris must battle the forces of love. And once he discovers the woman in his arms plans to be the mother of his child, it's not easy.

Rounding out the month, Carol Grace brings us a *Lonely Millionaire* who's looking for a mail-order bride. Liz Ireland turns up the laughter when a young woman finds herself playing *Mom for a Week*—with only her long-ago love to rescue her. And look for *The Man Who Changed Everything* from debut author Elizabeth Sites.

Until next month,

Happy reading!

Anne Canadeo
Senior Editor

Please address questions and book requests to:
Silhouette Reader Service
U.S.: 3010 Walden Ave., P.O. Box 1325, Buffalo, NY 14269
Canadian: P.O. Box 609, Fort Erie, Ont. L2A 5X3

LONELY
MILLIONAIRE

Carol Grace

Silhouette
R O M A N C E™
Published by Silhouette Books
America's Publisher of Contemporary Romance

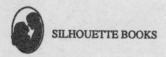

SILHOUETTE BOOKS

ISBN 0-373-19057-3

LONELY MILLIONAIRE

Printed in U.S.A.

CAROL GRACE

has always been interested in travel and living abroad. She spent her junior year in college in France and toured the world working on the hospital ship HOPE. She and her husband spent the first year and a half of their marriage in Iran, where they both taught English. Then, with their toddler daughter, they lived in Algeria for two years.

Carol says that writing is another way of making her life exciting. Her office is an Airstream trailer parked behind her mountaintop home, which overlooks the Pacific Ocean and which she shares with her inventor husband, their daughter, and their son.

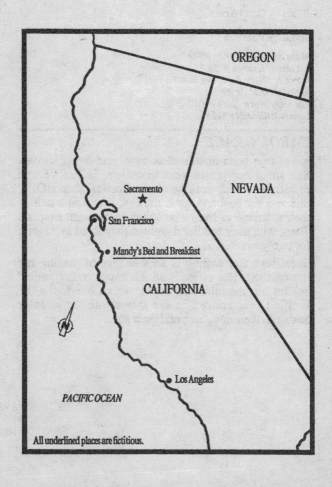

All underlined places are fictitious.

Chapter One

Wallpaper paste dripped onto Mandy Clayton's hair and her arms ached from holding them over her head. When the phone rang, she was on top of the ladder in the upstairs bathroom. Dropping her roller, she scrambled down the narrow rungs and ran downstairs.

"Miramar Inn," she said breathlessly into the phone.

"How's business?" her sister asked.

"Terrible. How was your flight?"

"Awful. Complete meal service for three hundred and fifty in two hours. Lecherous old men and crying babies. And you know that pilot I told you about?"

"The one with midnight blue eyes who invited you to his room for a game of Trivial Pursuit?"

"It was pursuit all right, but it wasn't trivial, *and* he's married. I hate this job. For two cents I'd quit and work for you."

"That's all I could afford to pay you," Mandy said, "and you'd be bored silly. You wouldn't meet any eligible men, either. They don't come to bed and breakfasts unless their wives or girlfriends drag them."

"I wish I had someone to drag to one. By the way, has my latest *Yukon Man* come yet?"

"I think so."

"Could you go get it and read me some of the personals? It might cheer me up."

"Laurie, I've got wallpaper paste all over my hands. You don't want me to smear it all over those gorgeous men, do you?"

"I'll wait while you wash your hands. I've got a twelve hour layover."

Mandy set the receiver down and went to wash her hands, muttering to herself that *she* didn't have twelve hours to kill, that someone might be trying to call right now and make reservations for one of her two lovely rooms overlooking the ocean in scenic Moss Beach, California.

Returning with magazine in hand, Mandy riffled quickly through the pages, skimming past bare-chested men flexing their muscles and flannel-shirted men with bulging biceps chopping wood until she came to a half-page ad with no picture at all.

"Here you go," she announced. "In *big, huge* letters— 'LONELY MILLIONAIRE seeks sensuous, understanding lady with good math skills to help me count my money.'"

"That's him, that's the one," Laurie said gleefully. "Tell me more."

"Well, he's a mining engineer who lives a million miles from nowhere. Are you sure that's what you want?"

"Not me. You. This one's perfect for you."

"Oh, no, he isn't. Leave me out of this. I have no interest in men. I thought you knew that."

"I know that one man told you he wasn't ready to make a commitment and then turned around and made one to your best friend. But that was three years ago. It's time to stop feeling sorry for yourself and start thinking of others. Others who are stuck in the wilds of the Yukon, a zillion miles from nowhere. Think of how much one letter would brighten this poor—I mean, *rich* man's lonely days."

Mandy stared at the ad. "You realize that this whole thing could be a joke, don't you?" she asked.

"If it is a joke then you've found a man with a sense of humor. Come on, just one letter. I *dare* you."

Mandy took a deep breath. She never could resist a dare. From the time Laurie dared her to jump out of the apple tree when she was ten and she broke her wrist to the time her sister had dared her to jump off the high dive at the high school pool and she'd smacked her stomach so hard it had left a red mark for days. Every one of those dares had turned out badly, and yet she still couldn't resist. There was something of the daredevil left in the thirty-two-year-old woman that she'd thought was long gone. But this time there was no danger of getting hurt, she told herself. The chances were this "Lonely Millionaire" would be deluged with letters and never write back.

"Okay," Mandy said. "You know how to get to me. But just one letter. That's all."

"Of course," Laurie said soothingly. "And while you're at it, you ought to take out an ad in *Yukon Man* yourself. For the inn, I mean. I bet those guys are always looking for a good place for R and R."

"That's a thought," Mandy said.

"A good thought. Now don't forget to write the letter."

When Laurie hung up, Mandy went back up the stairs to try to make the wallpaper stick to the wall. She wanted to finish before a guest checked in, but so far she had no reservations. Instead the bedrooms stood forlorn and empty, with their handmade quilts and starched damask curtains fluttering in the ocean breeze. If she were on R and R, she would come here, she thought, pausing in the doorway to admire the tiled fireplace already laid for a cozy fire, the padded window seats and the stacked bookshelves.

She was glad Laurie wasn't there to see her staring off into space. She might think Mandy *was* feeling sorry for herself. But why should she be when she had everything she wanted right here, a wonderful old house and a beautiful view?

She'd put the past behind her. She didn't need a man in her life, and if she did, answering personal ads was not the way to find one. She wished Laurie realized that. Those ads were written by weirdos, psychos and out-and-out liars. But she'd accepted the dare and she wouldn't back out now. One letter and that was it.

But the summer was foggy along the coast and Mandy had very few customers. She wrote her letter and to her surprise got one back almost immediately. Lonely Millionaire didn't sound like a weirdo, he sounded intelligent, funny and interesting. So interesting she wrote another letter and then another, until she found that she was looking forward to the mail with breathless anticipation.

The man was not only a rugged outdoorsman who could handle the Arctic weather and difficult living conditions, he seemed like a sensitive, caring kind of guy who sometimes expressed himself so beautifully it brought tears to her eyes. Other times he was outrageously funny and flippant and made her laugh out loud.

Lonely Millionaire's real name was Jack Larue and he was serious about looking for a wife. In fact, Mandy had the feeling he might possibly be considering her as a candidate... but she knew better than that. She'd been through that, through the hope and the disappointment, and she'd never let herself hope again. Still... if ever she did love again, it would be someone like Jack.

* * *

Fall came and the fog lifted and Mandy went back up the ladder in the bathroom to attack the wallpaper again. She closed the bathroom door and turned on a rented machine from the hardware store. Steam filled the air and the wallpaper dutifully began to curl around the edges. She picked up the scraper and hacked at the wall with a vengeance. Somewhere in the distance there was a knocking—no, a *pounding* on the front door.

Her pulse quickened. Could it be...? Was it possibly...? No, it couldn't be a guest, it must be the meter reader. She turned off the steamer, closed the door behind her and ran down the wide, varnished stairs to the front door.

"Coming," she called, sliding the last few feet on the soles of her cotton espadrilles and flinging the door open. It was... Miracle of miracles, it *was* a guest. No meter reader ever wore a bomber jacket and aviator sunglasses. She gave him her most dazzling smile, and he took off his glasses and stared as if she were a ghost appearing out of nowhere instead of a frazzled woman who was just breathless from running down the stairs.

She ran her damp palms down the sides of her jeans. Suddenly she was aware of her hair, steamed into a mass of frizz, her huge shirt stained with goo and her old blue jeans ripped at one knee. No wonder he was staring. He was wondering if he'd come to the right place. In her brochure she'd been photographed in a long skirt and a hand-knit sweater, looking calm and gracious. She cleared her throat and opened her arms.

"Welcome to Miramar Inn," she said. "I'm Mandy Clayton."

The man took a step forward. "Any vacancies?" he asked in a voice as deep as limestone.

Any vacancies? Did the tide come in every day? "Why, yes, I think so. Something overlooking the ocean...actually, everything overlooks the ocean. Would that be all right?"

"Sounds good."

"For how many nights?"

"I'm...not sure. Could I let you know on that?"

Mandy smoothed the wrinkles in her jeans, wishing she'd had time to slip into something more hostesslike, wishing she sounded more professional and not so desperate, as if he were the first guest to appear in weeks, which he was. "Of course."

She held the door open for him and he followed her inside to the living room, where he signed his name in her register—Adam Gray. Then she invited him to have a cup of coffee in the kitchen, where he stared out the window at the dark blue sea beyond the cliffs.

"Nice view," he observed. But his gaze left the ocean and shifted to her oversize shirt, her snug-fitting jeans and her untidy hair. She stood perfectly still and held her breath. A shiver ran up her spine despite the warmth of the sun streaming in the window. She wanted to say something, but her lips were numb. It was the shock of finding an unexpected guest on her front steps after all this time, she told herself firmly; and not the fact that he was the best looking man she'd seen in months, maybe ever.

"Decaf?" she said at last, grabbing a large white apron from the hook on the wall and wrapping it around her as if it were a shield from his penetrating gaze.

"Regular," he answered.

When the coffee was brewed she filled two mugs and pushed the kitchen door open with the toe of her canvas shoe. She was proud of her patio. The afternoon sun warmed the bricks she'd laid and the fence sheltered it from the brisk ocean breeze.

"I hope it isn't too cold out here for you," she said, putting the mugs on a small metal table.

He smiled and her heart did a double somersault. She'd never seen a smile transform a face like that. His sensuous mouth curved and laugh lines appeared at the corners of his eyes. She felt as if she'd said something wonderfully witty, but she didn't know what it was.

"Hardly. I just came down from the Yukon Territory, up near the Arctic Sea."

"The Yukon...as in *Yukon Man*?" she asked, stupefied.

"That's right. That's where I saw your ad."

"Oh, oh, of course. My ad." She didn't ask if he'd ever appeared in *Yukon Man* himself. It was obvious he wasn't the kind of man who needed to advertise for a woman. But if he did, he ought to be on the cover. He was everything the rugged Yukon man should be: granite-jawed with deep-set eyes that viewed the world with interest, and high cheekbones bronzed from the midnight sun. If only this was what her pen pal Jack looked like. But that was wishful thinking, and unworthy of someone who was more interested in character than outward appearances anyway. "This is a silly question," she continued, "but I don't suppose you know a Jack Larue up there in the Yukon?"

He smiled again and her knees threatened to buckle. She hoped he had no idea the effect that smile had on her. "Afraid not. It's a big territory."

"Oh...right. I know that. So, you're here on vacation?"

"Business actually. I'm a geologist and my home office is nearby in Menlo Park. I thought I'd take a few days off before I report, and soak up some California sunshine at the beach." He sat down in a chair next to the table and stretched his legs out. "Tell me, Mandy, how's business?"

He could have stayed for a week and not asked that question. It was the one question she didn't want to answer. "Actually, summer is our slow season," she confessed. "But things really pick up during the fall with the good weather." She crossed her fingers behind her back and sat down across from him.

"I'm lucky to get a room, then. The weather's great, the view's spectacular, and I guess there are some interesting things to see around here."

"Oh, absolutely." She beamed at him. Here was the perfect guest. He liked the place to begin with, and if he liked it maybe he would spread the word around the Yukon and more men would come and she'd be booked ahead of time, earn money and make a go of it. "In fact, I'll make a list of attractions for you, like the Winchester Mystery House, Great America and, of course, our own beach and tide pools."

"I was hoping you'd be able to show them to me in person," he said, looking at her intently over the rim of his coffee cup.

She paused. "Well, that depends . . ."

"On how busy you are. I understand that. It's just that I'm so bad at directions I'd probably get lost on my way out of your driveway."

"Even to the beach?"

He drew his eyebrows together, then pointed to the ocean straight ahead of them. "That way?" he inquired.

She nodded.

"I guess I could get that far by myself, but after that . . ."

"I'll see what I can do, Mr. Gray." He seemed to be coming on a little strong, this Adam Gray. Did bed-and-breakfast guests really expect the hostess to take them sightseeing? Maybe they did. Maybe she should. After all, she had nothing else to do that couldn't wait.

"Call me Adam," he said.

"Maybe you'd like to see your room, Adam," she suggested, pushing her chair back from the table.

He joined her a few minutes later in the living room with a leather overnight bag slung over his shoulder.

"You live here all alone?" he asked, following her up the stairs.

"My sister Laurie lives with me. But she's a flight attendant and she's out of town right now. She's the one who suggested I advertise in *Yukon Man,*" Mandy said. "She subscribes." She paused on the landing and looked at Adam over her shoulder.

He nodded. "I don't suppose you ever ... ?"

"Read it? No. And I'd never answer one of the ads. I don't suppose you would ever ... ?"

"Advertise myself? Not on your life. You know what kind of women you'd meet, pathological liars, schizophrenics ..."

"The same kind of men who advertise. It's really a shame our society has come to this," she agreed, coming to a stop at the upstairs landing.

He leaned against the smooth, polished railing. "Well, now that we have that out of the way, what kind of man *are* you looking for?"

"Me?" she asked, startled. "I'm not looking for anyone." She turned to face him. "What about you?"

"Me, either. Living in the Yukon is not conducive to long-term relationships. I know. I tried."

A tiny wrinkle formed in her forehead. "I'm sorry."

He put his hand on her arm. "Don't be. It's over now and it was a learning experience. I learned what's really important."

The touch of his hand sent signals to her brain that said, *Watch out.* But for the moment she chose to ignore them. "Which is ... ?" she prompted.

"Freedom, independence, excitement, adventure." His gaze locked on hers, and the words sunk in and stayed there. His hand stayed on her arm, too, the warmth radiating all the way through her body. Mandy's breath sat stuck in her throat. There was an aura about him, a magnetic field she'd stumbled into by mistake and couldn't get out of. She was supposed to be going somewhere, doing something, but she couldn't remember what it was.... Oh, yes. The room.

She pulled her arm away and turned around. "Right down here at the end of the hall," she said briskly. "I think you'll find everything you need. The bathroom's next door."

"Thanks."

She managed a smile, then hurried down the stairs to take refuge in the kitchen.

Chapter Two

Adam changed into shorts and a polo shirt in the bedroom he'd been given, ran downstairs and hit the beach running. It was exactly where she'd said it was, directly to the west and down the rickety wooden steps. His bare feet made wet prints in the narrow strip of sand. It was high tide and not a sign of the advertised tide pools was in sight. Everything else, however, was exactly as advertised. The house with the large, inviting bedrooms, views of the sea and extra-long beds with thick comforters, as well as the promise of delicious breakfasts to come. But he wasn't here for the bed or the breakfasts, he was here on a mission, and he couldn't let himself forget it.

He was here to check out Mandy Clayton for his friend Jack Larue. After a long, exhausting summer of wading through an avalanche of letters, Jack had narrowed the search for Miss Right down to two—Mandy Clayton and a former Miss Illinois. Since Jack was still at work back in the Yukon, and Adam had a business trip planned to Califor-

nia anyway, Adam had reluctantly agreed to take a look at
Mandy and make a brief report, while he was in the neigh-
borhood. Then Jack would know whether to pursue Miss
Illinois at full speed or make Mandy his target.

But Adam was hardly an impartial observer. He'd helped
Jack sort his mail and even written some letters for him.
Actually, he'd written all the letters to Mandy for him. After all, the guy had been swamped and he really wanted to
get married. Adam had noticed from the beginning that
Mandy's letters were a cut above everybody else's and he
had to admit it had made the summer months fly by antic-
ipating her responses. She was funny, charming, witty and
refreshingly honest. Or so he'd thought until she said she'd
never answer an ad in *Yukon Man* magazine.

On the other hand, he'd just heard himself deny that he
knew anyone named Jack Larue, who was his best friend.
So they'd each told one white lie. They were even. Except
for the fact that Jack wasn't a millionaire. He *planned* to be
a millionaire, right after he struck it rich in an abandoned
Klondike gold mine but he wasn't, as he claimed in his personal, a millionaire. Lonely, yes, but not wealthy—yet. Jack
maintained that the right woman wouldn't mind, she would
love him for himself and not his money. But Adam, who
was more skeptical about women, doubted it. If somebody
was inclined to answer an ad for a millionaire, she was going to be disappointed to find out he wasn't one.

He sat down on the wet sand and stared at the waves that
crashed against the shore. That was the one thing he was
supposed to find out. Was Mandy self-sufficient and self-
supporting, or was she really after Jack's millions that he
didn't have? And that wasn't all. There was a whole long list
of questions Jack wanted answered. He wondered how long
it would take to get the answers. He didn't have all week. He
had a meeting scheduled next week at the office. And he

hadn't counted on spending his vacation digging up facts for Jack.

He hadn't counted on Mandy looking as she did, either. She looked like sunshine and flowers, a breath of fresh sea air with her long legs and her rounded curves. When that door had opened and she'd stood there, he'd felt something so earthshaking he had known that it was Mandy Clayton. No question. He would have known her anywhere. If she'd suddenly appeared out of an Arctic blizzard, he would have recognized her. Only she was a hundred times better. Who could have expected she would have eyes the deep blue of the Pacific Ocean, or a dimple in one cheek that flashed when he least expected it, and honey-gold skin that looked as soft as silk?

Those were details that would interest Jack. They would interest any red-blooded American male. On the other hand, looks were important, but so were other things, and he had to get back and continue his investigation. He kicked up the sand with his toes and ran down the empty beach one more time, feeling the sun on his shoulders, the wind in his face, until his muscles ached and his heart pounded. Then he climbed the wooden steps back to the house.

There was a shower at the top of the steps just inside the fence, a small foot shower that he turned on to rinse his feet. He wouldn't want to track any sand onto her varnished floors. It was a great house, lovingly cared for, so welcoming, waiting patiently with no one there to appreciate it. Almost like Mandy herself, living alone on the edge of a cliff. She'd said business was good, but he doubted it. She hadn't even looked in her calendar to see if she had room for him.

He walked through the kitchen door and up the stairs toward the bedroom. Music reverberated through the house. He recognized the B52's and he heard her singing along with them to the song "Roam." Roam, it was his own personal philosophy of life. If you kept on roaming, you would never be anywhere long enough to miss it when you left. He paused outside the bathroom door and knocked. The music stopped abruptly. She opened the door a crack and peered out at him. Billows of steam obscured her oval face and tall, curvaceous body.

"Sorry," she said. "I'll be out of here in a minute. I was trying to finish up before you got back."

He craned his head to look inside. "Go ahead. Finish your shower. I didn't mean to interrupt."

"I'm not taking a shower. Why would I be taking a shower with my clothes on? I'm steaming the paper off the walls." She pulled the door open. "See?"

Through the steam he saw a room with a porcelain clawfoot tub along the wall. There were piles of thick towels stacked on shelves and hand-painted tiles in peach and moss green around the sink. And in the middle of it all was a stepladder, with scraps of wallpaper scattered underneath it.

He also saw tiny rivulets of perspiration trickling down her face, and her T-shirt was clinging damply to her breasts. He noticed that she'd changed into shorts, revealing smooth, shapely legs, but he forgot to notice the walls. Instead he stepped into the room and closed the door behind him, feeling an acceleration of his pulse rate.

"Can I help?"

"Oh, no, you're a guest," she protested, backing into the ladder.

"It would make me feel better about barging in on you without a reservation."

She picked up a metal scraper and studied him carefully as if he'd applied for a difficult job, one that she doubted he could handle. "Well..." she said dubiously.

"Don't you want your guests to feel at home?" he asked, taking the scraper out of her hand.

Instead of answering, she braced the ladder against the wall and climbed to the top, putting some distance between them. "Where is your home?" she asked.

"Wherever they send me," he answered, looking up. His gaze followed her long, bare legs, her shirt that hung wide and loose. For a brief second he had a breathtaking view of her firm, ripe breasts unencumbered by a bra. He took a deep breath and went down on his knees to attack the wall with the scraper. And while he was there, he said a prayer for strength enough to resist the temptation to come on to Jack's girl. It would be wrong, unethical, inadvisable and *definitely* distract him from his goal. "I really don't have a home," he added.

"I wouldn't like that," she mused, sending a strip of loose paper floating down to land on his shoulder. She mumbled an apology and he smiled, brushing it away easily.

"Most women wouldn't. Moving around, that is. Women are nesters. Men are migrators."

"Is that right?" she asked. "I don't think you can put people in categories, like birds. Some men want to settle down. Some women are always on the move, like my sister. She's in New York this week, and Toledo next week. But that doesn't mean she doesn't want to settle down, if she found the right man."

"Maybe she'll meet someone on the plane. If she's half as attractive as you are." A blob of dried wallpaper paste fell on his head and he jerked his head up. "What was that for, can't you take a compliment?"

"I prefer honesty," she said.

His ears burned. Everyone preferred honesty, only sometimes it just wasn't possible. So far he'd only lied to her once, and maybe he could get through the week without another fabrication.

"Anyway," she continued. "She meets lots of men on planes, but you have no idea how many men are out there pretending to be something they're not."

Like Jack, he thought, keeping his head down. Pretending to be a millionaire. He'd told him not to do it, but Jack said it was just a way of catching their attention, of standing out from the crowd of personal ads. He was right. He'd caught their attention all right, the attention of hundreds of women. Was Mandy the one in a hundred, the one for Jack? Or was she too good for Jack?

How was he going to find out? *By spending as much time as possible with her this week,* he answered himself too eagerly, *by finding out everything he could about her, including how she felt about Jack, if possible.*

Mandy rubbed her hands on a damp towel and decided to put an end to the work party. Not that it wasn't enjoyable to have someone share the work and discuss the difference between men and women, but she had other things to do. And she'd discovered that she'd been peeling the same spot for the past fifteen minutes while spending too much of the time looking down at the back of Adam's head. She'd even wondered how his dark hair would feel if she ran her fingers through it. Definitely not appropriate thoughts for a hostess to feel about her one and only single male guest.

No wonder she couldn't keep her mind and her eyes off him. She'd been alone too long, without guests, without men in her life. She started down the ladder and he steadied it for her. But instead of holding the ladder, he moved his hands to her bare legs, sending tremors up the sensitive skin of her inner thighs. The ladder shook, her knees wobbled and his hands moved to her hips and stayed there. She landed on the floor with a thud and turned to face him. The steam swirled around them, creating their own little biosphere. Their eyes met and held for a long moment.

"Look," he said, "everyone prefers honesty, but sometimes they have their reasons for not telling the truth. Sometimes it's just to spare other people's feelings, like when someone asks what you think of their new baby or their new car. You don't want to say it looks like Winston Churchill or it gets lousy mileage. You can't tell me you haven't told a little white lie once or twice?"

He took the towel out of her hand and put it down on a ladder rung, holding her hands in his. She looked into his eyes and immediately got a picture of a tough Arctic man who radiated rugged sensuality from every pore, and who could see into the depths of her soul. Someone who knew that she'd lied about never answering an ad in *Yukon Man*. She had to get out of this small, steamy bathroom, but she couldn't seem to move, couldn't even tear her eyes away from his.

"Of course I've told little white lies," she confessed breathlessly. "After all, I'm only human." Never before had she felt so human than at that moment. It was a combination of the heat, the guilt, and the close proximity of this man who made her feel like a melting marshmallow over a hot fire.

"I noticed," he said in a deep voice. He pulled her close to him, until the tips of her breasts grazed his chest. The steam had given her skin a dewy sheen and he wanted to reassure her, tell her she hadn't done anything wrong, and show her just how human he found her. But not with words, with action. He wanted to release all his pent-up emotion by kissing her until she couldn't think, couldn't speak. Until he'd tasted those soft lips and she'd had a taste of what he had to offer....

But he wasn't there to kiss his best friend's prospective fiancée. He'd already gone too far. Reluctantly he let go of her hands and opened the door behind him. A rush of cool air blew in and dissipated the steam and the mood.

"I'll clear this stuff out of here," she said, folding the ladder. "Then it's all yours. Thanks for the help."

He reached for the ladder and his fingers brushed hers. She bent over to unplug the steamer. "Where shall I put this?" he asked.

"Downstairs at the back door, if you wouldn't mind.

He hoisted the ladder to his shoulder and paused in the doorway. "What time is sherry in the parlor?"

"What?"

"I was reading your brochure in my room. Sherry time is where you meet the other guests and the hostess tells you interesting anecdotes about the house."

"Oh, right. I almost forgot." She looked at her watch, embarrassed that she'd forgotten what her own brochure said. The combination of him and the steam had definitely fogged her brain. "How about four o'clock?"

He nodded. "It will give me a chance to take a shower and change."

Absently she smoothed a piece of wallpaper with her fingers and let her gaze travel over his wrinkled shorts, his muscular thighs and bare feet. Then she brought her eyes back to his face. He was studying her intently. What did he want? What was he looking for? Was this gorgeous man really just in search of some California sunshine?

"I can tell you about the house," she said, "but I'm afraid you won't get to meet anyone but me." She smiled self-consciously. "Not tonight, anyway."

He smiled back, sending a rush of warmth through her body. Then he carried the ladder down the stairs while she put the bathroom back in order. She wondered idly if Adam had ever considered entering into another long-term relationship. Not with her, of course, but with someone else who was also employed in the Yukon, a welder maybe, or a pipe fitter.

She was still wondering about Adam Gray as she clipped the hedge out in front of the house that afternoon. And she was still wearing her old shirt and shorts when the car pulled up. Not someone on their way to the beach, not someone who was looking for the restaurant down the road, but surprise, surprise, someone—*someones*—who were looking for her, for the Miramar Inn.

She practically swept them up into her arms, all three of them: Mr. Richard Davis, Marilyn Davis and little Jeremy Davis, age eighteen months. She proudly showed them to the other bedroom, the one with the master bath, and set up a crib for the little boy. They loved the room, they loved the view, they loved the fact that she accepted children, and they loved the idea of sherry in the parlor at four.

Mandy hummed to herself as she showered in the small, downstairs bathroom next to her bedroom. Miramar Inn was full, it was occupied, she was on her way to success. She dressed carefully in the same outfit she'd worn in her brochure picture. Not for luck, not so she'd be recognized as the hostess, but simply because it was the only nice outfit she had. A long cotton skirt and a hand-knit sweater with a pattern of wild roses on it.

With Laurie's hair dryer she tried to tame the wild mess that was her hair with only moderate success. If only Laurie were here to do it for her. But if Laurie were here, Adam would be all over her like glue. Laurie's hair was always manageable, she was trim and slender, looked great in a uniform or anything else. Mandy reminded herself that the only reason Adam was giving her a second glance was because she was the only woman for miles around.

But that knowledge didn't detract from her pleasure in having a full house tonight. As it neared four o'clock she went to the kitchen. She unwrapped a package of crackers and took a duck liver pâté and a round of Brie from the refrigerator. Then she piled pears and apples into a bowl and loaded everything onto a tray.

When she walked into the front room balancing the tray in her hands, she saw Adam was there ahead of her in khakis and a blue oxford-cloth shirt, looking at her old photographs on the wall. He turned and gave her a long, appreciative look and took the tray from her hands.

Again the brush of his fingers against hers, and this time she was sure it wasn't an accident. Electricity crackled in the air. She couldn't blame it on the dry air or the carpet. The air was damp and the Oriental carpet was threadbare. A current rippled through her body and sent a message that said, *Beware, this is your second warning!*

Adam's hair was still damp from the shower and his skin looked as if he'd scrubbed it with the loofah she'd placed in the bathroom. He smelled like the soap she'd left out. Wild blackberry—or was it wild cherry? Now she understood why they called it that. It made her wild just thinking about him rubbing it all over his well-toned body. With shaking hands she set the decanter of sherry out on the sideboard along with the glasses.

"Help yourself," she said, not trusting herself to pour any drinks. Where were the Davises? Why didn't they come and fill the silence with their conversation and their questions?

Adam turned back to the pictures on the wall. "Is this your family?" he asked.

She managed to slosh some sherry into a glass for herself and walked over to the wall. "Yes, that's us. I was four and my sister, Laurie, was two. We lived in Ohio."

"Anything more recent?"

"Over here. Here's Laurie in her uniform." She held her breath. When he saw how beautiful Laurie was, he'd probably stay around until she came back. That was the effect Laurie had on men. And it wouldn't surprise Mandy. She was used to having men drop her when they met someone else, witness Todd and her best friend.

But he passed right by the photo with only a perfunctory comment and went on to the other pictures while she explained them to him—uncles, aunts, cousins at picnics, parties and reunions.

"I envy you," he said, examining an old photograph of her grandparents.

"What for? You can get frames and hang pictures of your family, can't you?"

"I don't have any. We moved around a lot when I was a kid, and we traveled light. And even if I had them, where would I hang them?"

"Wherever they send you. There are walls, aren't there?" Mandy asked.

"There are walls on drilling platforms on the North Slope, but you don't get much chance to look at them. They keep you busy sinking pipe into the bottom of the sea."

"Is that where you're going, to a drilling platform?" Mandy asked, surprised.

"That's the plan. That's what I asked for. But you never know. I've got an appointment with my boss next week. I'll find out then," Adam said.

At that moment the Davises finally joined them, eighteen-month-old Jeremy tottering straight for the sherry decanter. Adam grabbed it from the table just in time and poured drinks. Mandy shot him a grateful look and introduced them.

"What a wonderful place to live," Marilyn Davis gushed to Adam while Mandy offered Jeremy a cracker.

"Yes, it is," he agreed, "but..."

"You two are such gracious hosts," she continued. "That's what makes a bed and breakfast."

"Can I get Jeremy some apple juice?" Mandy asked, not bothering to explain that Adam and she weren't anything at all.

"Wonderful," his mother said. Mandy left the room to get the juice, and Marilyn turned to Adam. "Can you recommend someplace for dinner?" she asked.

For some reason he found he didn't want to tell her that he was a guest, too, and that he had no idea of where her family should go eat. "What kind of food do you like?" he asked instead.

"Seafood," she said.

"You'll have to ask Mandy about that." Out of the corner of his eye he saw Jeremy sitting in front of the bookcase removing the books, one by one. When Mandy came back with a tumbler for the little boy, Marilyn was spreading cheese on a cracker.

"Your husband told me to ask you for a restaurant recommendation."

Mandy's eyes widened. "My *what?*"

He bit back a grin.

"We're looking for a quiet place that serves seafood. It says in your brochure..."

"Yes, I know just the place." When she recovered her composure she gave them the directions to the Seadrift, a few miles away. They had excellent food and a beautiful view.

"I don't see how the view could be any better than yours." Richard Davis spoke for the first time, looking out the side window at the sun setting over the blue-gray Pacific.

"It isn't, but the food is," she said, watching Jeremy smash a cracker into the carpet with the heel of his foot. She swallowed hard to keep from saying anything.

"Oh, yes," Marilyn said taking the chair next to the window, "about the baby-sitting service?"

"Baby-sitting?"

"I read in the brochure..."

"Of course. I haven't had many children so I almost forgot." There was a long silence while her mind went absolutely blank. Where on earth would she ever find a baby-sitter?

"We'd be glad to take care of Jeremy for you," she heard Adam say, and she whirled around to look at him. He shrugged as if to say, What choice have you got?

"He may cry for a few minutes," Marilyn said, "but it won't last long. He's really very good."

"Don't worry about a thing," Adam said reassuringly, and Mandy shot him a desperate look.

How could he tell them not to worry about a thing? He would probably retire to his room and leave Mandy with this eighteen-month-old terror who'd start screaming the minute his parents left him. But what choice did Mandy have? Regardless of Adam's offer she *had* advertised baby-sitting. That she'd been caught off guard didn't matter. Mandy sipped her sherry and smiled brightly. She'd get Adam for this later. For now she had to "hostess."

And screaming was exactly what the little boy did. Mandy brought shiny copper pots from the kitchen and sat down on the floor to play with him later, but he refused to play. She gave him spoons and metal measuring cups, but he ignored them. He stood in the middle of the room and opened his mouth and yelled at the top of his lungs. Mandy tried to pick him up, but he stomped on the floor and threw the cups across the room. His face was bright red and the tears streamed down his cheeks. Clearly he was not happy at being left with these people who were not his parents.

Still on the floor, Mandy leaned against the overstuffed chair and threw her head back on the cushion. "This was your idea," she yelled at Adam over the din. "You offered. Do something."

Adam kneeled on the floor and banged two pots together, but Jeremy wasn't interested. He threw himself on the floor and continued screaming.

"Maybe he's hungry," Adam suggested.

"What'll we give him?"

"Whatever we're having for dinner."

"We?"

"It says in the brochure..."

Mandy crawled on her hands and knees to where Adam had taken refuge against the wall so she wouldn't have to shout. "No, it doesn't. It says bed and breakfast, not bed and dinner. I don't do dinners."

He didn't argue. He went back to the little boy, lifted him by the elbows and carried him into the kitchen, with Mandy following close behind. "Give him something—anything," Adam said. "If you can get him quiet, I'll cook dinner."

Mandy grabbed a blueberry muffin from the freezer and popped it into the microwave oven, then installed Jeremy at the table by stacking phone books on a chair. His screams had turned to snuffles, but he still wasn't a happy camper. She broke off a corner of the muffin and held it up in front of him. He took it, looked at it, and threw it across the floor.

"Not much of a testimonial to your baking skills, is it?" Adam remarked with a grin.

Mandy retrieved the crumbs and gave Adam a look of desperation. "Are you really going to make dinner?" she asked hopefully.

"That depends," he said, his head in the freezer. "Aha, chicken. You're in luck. After ten years in the bush I am known as the best chef in the Arctic Circle."

"Is there much competition for that honor?" she inquired, taking a chair next to Jeremy and preparing another bite of muffin to pop into his mouth.

Adam tossed the frozen chicken onto the drainboard. "Plenty," he assured her.

"Then how come no one's snapped you up by now, or have they?" she inquired casually. If they had, why wouldn't they be here together, here at this romantic bed and breakfast? Still, it didn't hurt to ask.

"Women don't like living miles from the nearest shopping mall."

"What about someone who already lives up there, who works with you?"

"Nobody works with me, except...one other person, and he's a man. How would you like it, living in the Arctic with only your dog team for company?"

"I don't know," she said thoughtfully. It wasn't the first time she'd wondered about it. Ever since she'd been writing to Jack, she'd tried to picture herself there. Even though Jack told her he was planning to leave the Yukon and work somewhere else. "What's it like?" she asked. Even though she knew what it was like from Jack's colorful letters, she wanted to hear somebody else's opinion.

"It's cold, it's bleak, but it's beautiful, too. We've got Mt. Logan covered with snow even in summer, the Yukon River rushing to the sea. And it's so quiet you can hear the snow fall."

She looked out the kitchen window as the sun dipped into the ocean, leaving behind a magical green flash. "It's pretty quiet right here," she observed.

"As long as you keep your little friend's mouth full," he said with a glance at the boy who was scattering crumbs in a widening circle around his chair.

She nodded and gave the boy a drink of juice. She watched while Adam defrosted the chicken in her microwave oven, and then chopped onions and celery, admiring his smooth, efficient motions, his large, capable hands. The same hands that peeled wallpaper.... How could she charge him anything after he'd done all this work?

Was he sorry he'd checked into a B and B only to find himself working harder than he did as an engineer? He didn't look sorry. He looked as though he was concentrating on the preparations for dinner. And after all, he *was* the one who had volunteered them as baby-sitters.

"Why did you tell those people we were married?" she asked suddenly.

He threw the onions into a large frying pan. "I didn't. They just assumed."

"You could have told them we *weren't* married."

"So could you."

"Oh, well. They'll be gone tomorrow and we'll never see them again," she said in a rush. It wouldn't be too good an idea to explore this with him. She picked Jeremy up off his makeshift seat and balanced him on her hip. "What are you making?" she asked, looking over Adam's shoulder.

Before he could answer, the phone rang.

She went to the counter and picked up the receiver. "Miramar Inn," she said. Then she held it out to Adam. "It's for you."

Adam turned off the front burner and frowned. Only one person knew where he was and he didn't want to hear from him right now.

"Yes?" he answered warily, mouthing a silent "thank you" to Mandy for having passed him the phone.

"Adam, old friend. How's it going? Was that her? What's she like?"

"I really couldn't say," he said brusquely.

"Oh, I get it. She's right there with you."

"Obviously," Adam said through clenched teeth. "I'm in the middle of something right now. Could I call you back later?"

"Wait a minute. I can't stand the suspense. Just tell me if she's as good as I imagined. Can't you just do that, just say yes or no?"

"Yes."

"Yes. What does that mean? Can't you be more specific?"

"No."

"No, she's not what we thought? Or, no, you can't be specific?" Jack's voice rose. Adam couldn't blame him for being frustrated, but what did he have to do to explain that he couldn't talk?

Out of the corner of his eye he saw Mandy wave to him and go out the back door to the yard, holding Jeremy against her shoulder. When the door closed firmly behind her, he turned his back to the window and growled into the phone.

"Okay, she just went outside. What do you want to know?"

"Everything."

"I haven't got time for everything. She's nice."

"Nice? That's all?"

"She's nice-looking, too."

"On a scale of ten."

"I don't know, eight, nine, maybe." Liar, she was a ten-plus. What was wrong with him?

"Is she interested in starting a family? Does she object to cigar smoke? Is she after my money?"

"Slow down, Jack. I just got here, I don't want to come on too strong, she'll get suspicious."

"When can you find out?"

"I don't know. It's going to take longer than I thought."

"What am I supposed to tell Julie from Illinois? She's getting anxious. She wants to come up here."

"Stall her. Tell her it's going to take longer than you thought. I'll call you when I learn anything. But I can't just barge in here and ask a lot of questions, not unless you want me to tell her who I am."

"No, don't do that. Then we'll never find out if she's for real or not."

The back door opened and Mandy came in with Jeremy toddling behind her.

"Well, thanks for calling. Talk to you later," Adam said, and hung up. He looked at Mandy before he went back to the stove to add a dash of cooking wine to the mixture.

"Never give out your phone number when you're on vacation," he said. "Some people just won't leave you alone."

"A friend?"

"An associate who had a problem with a piece of equipment."

"Oh."

"I found some stuff for a salad in your refrigerator," he said, serving up two heaping bowls of crisp lettuce with an oil and vinegar dressing.

"It looks wonderful." She picked Jeremy off the floor where he was chasing a lost blueberry. She put him back on the stack of phone books and unfolded her napkin.

Adam set the salad bowls on the table, along with a small bowl of rice for Jeremy, and sat down across from them.

"How are things up there in the Yukon?" she asked.

"Long days and short nights. Hard to sleep, hard to work. Too much time to think," he observed. "And worry."

"Can't your friend...I mean, your associate, get away?"

"Not while I'm gone. We're a two-man team."

"I guess he misses you," she said, chewing thoughtfully.

"You could say that. Or you could say he misses having somebody to listen to him. Anyone would do."

"You're a good listener?"

He leaned forward. "Just try me," he said with a gleam in his eye.

She gulped and tore her gaze away from Adam's. She imagined he'd be a good listener, she thought he'd probably be good at anything he did.

Adam approached Jeremy from across the table with a heaping spoonful of rice in his hand. When the little boy opened his mouth, Adam shoveled it in and gave Mandy a triumphant grin.

The grin faded fast when Jeremy spit the rice out onto the table. Mandy shook her head and mopped it up. "So much for your reputation as the premier chef of the Arctic Circle," she teased. "I hope this doesn't get back to the Yukon."

He shook his head. "Remind me not to have children," he said.

Mandy offered the boy another sip of juice. "A lot of men want children," she observed, thinking of Jack, who'd confessed, in one of his letters that he wanted at least half a dozen.

"They do, why?" he asked.

"To carry on the family name, to have a stake in the future, all the usual reasons."

"Well maybe they need a few days with Jeremy here to think things over. Before they make any rash decisions."

"Did you, before you got here, I mean, want to have children?"

"Yes. Right up to a few minutes ago, I'd planned to have an even dozen. But since I've given up on women, it's probably just as well I changed my mind." He gave her a teasing grin and reached across the table to catch Jeremy before his forehead landed in his bowl of rice. Jeremy wasn't hungry but the poor little guy was definitely tired out.

Adam stood and lifted Jeremy into his arms.

"I'll put him to bed," Mandy whispered, and got to her feet.

Adam nodded and gently handed him to her. "Do you have any candles?" he asked as she shifted the child to her shoulder.

"On the bottom shelf," she said, pointing to the pantry. "In case of power outages. But I don't think we'll need them tonight," she said over her shoulder.

He watched her walk out of the room with the boy's head bobbing against her shoulder. Then he went looking for the candles and holders in the walk-in pantry. As he lit the wicks he thought that he knew who she meant by "a lot of men." Jack made no secret of wanting a big family. It was Jack who she was thinking of. It was Jack, with his scintillating letters, all of which were written by Adam, who was his rival.

"We may not need the candles tonight," he muttered to himself, "but we need something." Something to exorcise the presence of Jack, unseen and unspoken of, that great correspondent, that thoughtful, sensitive son-of-a-gun. "Sorry, old buddy. But I'm here and you're not. Tonight's my night and not yours."

Chapter Three

Mandy tiptoed down the stairs and into the kitchen. With the dim light and the delicious aroma coming from the stove, she hardly recognized her own kitchen. She paused in the doorway to accustom herself to the flickering candlelight.

Adam left the stove, went to meet her and bowed low. He had a dish towel draped over his arm. "Dinner for one?" he inquired in a seductive voice.

She nodded and he kissed her hand. His lips were warm. She felt a shiver of anticipation go up her spine.

"And where is *monsieur* tonight?" he asked in a deep voice.

"He, uh, decided to retire early," she murmured. "Perhaps he had a bit too much to drink."

"Ah," he said with a knowing wink. "The apple juice will do it every time. Your usual table?" He pulled her chair out for her.

"Do you have something else, farther from the kitchen?" She looked over her shoulder at the old-fashioned stove, wrinkling her nose just slightly.

"If I had only known. I just gave that table away."

"Gave it away?" she inquired, unfolding her napkin.

"Yes, to the Goodwill. Such a worthy organization. They were here this afternoon asking for donations. May I take your order?" He bent low over her shoulder, exuding a suave, debonair charm that was totally phony. After all, he was a rugged Yukon man, and yet... and yet... His hand brushed the nape of her neck and chills raced up and down her back at the same time heat rushed to her head.

"I—I..." she stammered.

"May I make a suggestion?" he asked, so close that she could feel his breath warming her cheek. "Have the chef. I mean, the chef's special. If you don't, he'll be very unhappy, and when the chef is unhappy..."

"I understand," she said, tilting her head just slightly in his direction until his mouth was only inches away. His lips hovered over hers, his gaze locked on hers. The distance between melted away and his lips brushed hers, just hinting at the hunger there.

She twisted the napkin in her lap. She knew it was wrong, but she couldn't help it, she wanted more. She wanted a kiss. A real kiss.

He tilted her chin with his thumb. "You're radiant tonight," he said, gazing into her eyes.

She lowered her lashes. "It must be the candlelight," she murmured.

He shook his head. It wasn't the candlelight that made her skin glow and her eyes shine. It was her. She was lovely with her curly hair in tendrils around her face and the candlelight reflected in her eyes. He dropped his hand from her face. "As you can see, we're overbooked."

She looked around the room. "Really?"

"Yes, it's always like this. Packed."

"Don't I wish," she said.

"Ever since the new chef arrived. So, I was wondering..." He picked up a curl from the nape of her neck and wound it around his finger. It was soft and silky, just as he'd known it would be. "Wondering if you would mind sharing your table?"

She felt his fingers laced in her hair and she exhaled a sigh of pure pleasure. The man knew what he was doing. He had magic in his hands and he was using it to tantalize her. She sat up straight and he let go.

"No, of course not. Depending on who it is, of course."

He moved to the other side of the table and gave her a slow smile. "It's someone who would like to get to know you better—me."

"You?" She studied his face, all planes and angles in the light from the single candle. "Well, all right," she agreed, feeling the corners of her mouth tilt upward to return his smile. "This *is* an unusual place."

Unusual, yes, to be a guest in her own kitchen, to be swept off her feet by this rugged stranger.

"First, our house wine," he said, holding the gallon jug of red wine as carefully as a fine vintage.

She lifted her glass and he filled it. "Nothing extraordinary, you understand," he said, "but it may amuse you."

She took a small sip and swirled it around in her glass. "Yes," she agreed. "I can see the humor in it."

"And now for the main course." He went to the stove and in a few minutes he had heaped some savory concoction onto two plates. Then he shoved another chair to the small oak breakfast table and sat down across from her.

She took a bite and tasted hot and spicy chicken served on a bed of fluffy rice. "What is it?" she asked.

"We call it chicken surprise. The surprise is we never know how it's going to turn out. I hope you like it."

"I do. I don't suppose the chef would share his recipe?"

"Not a chance, because there isn't one."

They ate in companionable silence. Mandy was enjoying the novelty of eating someone else's cooking, of eating something that wasn't breakfast. And when he wasn't looking, she studied the face of her companion and wondered if this was really happening.

He looked up suddenly and caught her staring at him. "What's wrong?"

She looked away. What was wrong was that there was nothing wrong. It was all too wonderful. He was too nice, too good-looking, too virile, too good a cook—she set her fork down. She had to know now. Before it was too late. Before she lost her head. "I was just wondering about your wife."

"What wife?" he asked.

"The one who...who..."

"Who walked out when she saw there was no decent shopping or hair stylist in the Yukon?" There was a note of bitterness in his voice that made her wish she hadn't asked, wish that she hadn't spoiled the mood.

"Sorry, it's none of my business."

"That's all right," he said. "It was my fault."

"Your fault for not providing a mall or a hairdresser?"

"My fault for getting married."

"Couldn't you have transferred?" she asked.

"I tried to, I'm still trying."

"But to a drilling platform. That would make it hard for any woman to share your life," she said with a frown.

"That would make it impossible," he said firmly.

"I see," she said thoughtfully. And she did see. At least he was up front about what he wanted, and it was better that she understand that right now.

He got to his feet and refilled her wineglass. "Enough about me," he said. "What are you doing out here on the edge of nowhere with no guests and no husband? Or is he out catching fish for tomorrow's breakfast?"

She shook her head. "No husband. I only fall for men who don't want to make commitments. Laurie says it's because I'm afraid to make one myself."

"What does she know about it?"

"She knows me pretty well. She says I won't compromise, either."

"Will you?"

"There's nothing to compromise when the man you've been going with for three years decides to take the plunge and marry your best friend." Her eyes suddenly filled with tears. Why on earth did she have to tell him the awful truth? He wasn't interested. He didn't care. He was just making conversation. She'd come all the way to this out-of-the-way locale to forget, and here she was dredging up the past the minute she found a sympathetic ear.

The next thing she knew she'd be crying on his shoulder. And what a shoulder to cry on, she thought, measuring the width of his shoulders through blurry eyes. She pushed her chair back from the table intending the clear away the dishes and put an end to this conversation. There wasn't a man in the world who wanted someone dampening his shirt over the guy who got away.

But before she could get up, he stood and rested a hand on her shoulder, a strong, warm hand that exerted just the right amount of pressure to keep her where she was.

"You're not leaving before dessert?" he said with mock outrage. "Do you have no feelings for the pastry chef?"

"Does he . . . does it come with the dinner?" she asked, feeling the warmth from his hand radiate to the vicinity of her heat.

"*Everything* is included," he assured her with a grin. "Including a shoulder to cry on," he added as if he'd read her mind.

She looked up and he cupped her face in his hands. Her eyes met his and she saw sympathy and understanding and something else flash for just a second. Something that might have been desire. He pulled her up to face him and she knew he was going to kiss her. This time it would be no brush of the lips, this time she'd meet him halfway, maybe more. And she would have, if the front door hadn't opened and the Davises hadn't called to them from the living room. She reached for the light switch and suddenly reality took over. The kitchen was only a kitchen, the table was old and scarred, and she, the proprietor of a bed and breakfast, was dining with a guest and letting herself get carried away.

As for Adam, he was staring at her as if he'd just heard an alarm bell ring.

"Thanks for the dinner," she said, smoothing her skirt, trying to pretend nothing had happened. Nothing had, except in her imagination. "I'll clean up after I say good-night to the Davises."

"No, you won't. I'll clean up after I say good-night and tell them what I think of their son."

"Don't you dare," Mandy whispered.

"Hello? Anyone home?" came the voice of Marilyn Davis. She burst through the door, her husband a step behind her, eyes sweeping across the kitchen to the piles of pots and pans in the sink, the table set for two, the candle dripping wax on the table.

"Oh, I'm sorry, we've interrupted your romantic little supper for two. That's so sweet. I hope when we're married as long as you two..." She paused. "How long did you say you'd been married?"

"We didn't say," Adam said smoothly.

"I hope we'll be as much in love as you two."

"Does it show?" Adam asked innocently.

Mandy blushed and hustled the Davises back into the living room with Adam a few steps behind her. Why didn't he go to bed? Why didn't he let *her* be the hostess? Why didn't one of them tell this woman that they weren't married?

"How was your dinner?" Mandy said to break the silence once they were all in the living room.

"Wonderful. It was everything you said it was." Marilyn Davis unbuttoned her jacket. "And how was Jeremy?"

Before she could answer, Adam broke in. "Very lively kid you've got there, with a great pair of lungs. Has he shown an interest in opera?"

"Not yet," his mother admitted.

"Well, I wouldn't be surprised if he had a great career ahead of him, would you, Mandy?"

"I wouldn't be surprised at anything. He's such a fine boy. He went to bed a few hours ago. All tuckered out," she said with a polite smile.

"We can't thank you enough," Marilyn said, and they finally went upstairs to bed.

Adam stood there, watching them go. Mandy could understand why he didn't go up immediately, since they were under the impression that they were married. But how long was he going to stand there looking at her as if she was the evening's entertainment?

"Where were we?" he inquired, his eyes lingering on the soft swell of her breasts under the hand-knit sweater. "I remember," he said with a gleam in his eyes. "We were going to have dessert."

Mandy brushed her hand across her forehead. *Oh, no, we aren't.* That was all she needed, to go back into that candlelit room and have him ply her with more food and drink. He'd weakened her resistance, he'd made her want to believe in love and romance again. He'd made her want to feel his arms around her, his lips on hers. He'd turned her kitchen into a romantic French bistro and himself into a dashing, romantic rogue. Which perhaps he was, even in the bright living room light. The light that let her see him for what he was—a rugged outdoorsman with a suave manner that he could turn on to make her feel soft and warm and desirable. A dangerous combination.

Adam realized the spell was broken. The evening had come to a crashing, jolting halt, and he felt deflated. He could have gone on all night, alternating coffee with wine and dessert and bantering with this bewitching, bewildering woman. He hadn't had so much fun in years.

He'd forgotten how much fun women were. Or maybe he'd never known. He could have sworn he wasn't missing anything. He'd thought he had it all. Or that he would once he got his new assignment, up where the wind took your breath away and the waves threatened to sweep you over the edge of the platform.

Looking at Mandy in the candlelight, though, had almost taken his breath away a few times and if he stayed there much longer he might be in more danger of being swept away than on one of those platforms. She was right. It was time to break up the party.

He took her by the shoulders and turned her around to face her room. "You go to bed," he said firmly. "I'll clean up. I'm the one who made the mess."

"No, you won't," she protested. "You're the guest." She twisted out of his hold and turned to face him.

"Then I get to do what I want."

"All right," she said.

The look in her eyes made his heart pound. There was hope and desire there, flickering and burning as brightly as any candle. She knew what he wanted. She wanted it, too, but neither would admit it, or make the first move. He would have, but reality had already intruded. She was, or would be, Jack's girl. Not his.

"See you tomorrow," he said. "Wake me in time for breakfast."

"I'll do that."

* * *

But she didn't do it until after the Davises had had their eggs Benedict, their freshly squeezed juice and their apple-bran muffins at her dining room table and had left with more promises to recommend the place to everyone they knew. Then and only then did she climb the stairs and knock hesitantly on Adam's door. There was no answer.

Worried, she opened the door just a crack. A shaft of sunlight picked up the colors in the blue-and-white Navaho rug. The sea sparkled in the distance outside the large windows. Her eyes traveled to the handmade quilt in a tangled heap on the bed. A pillow sat where his head should be. Was he still there, or had he sneaked out early that morning to avoid any further entanglement with his weepy, sentimental hostess?

"Adam?" she called softly, tiptoeing into the room.

The blankets moved. He sat up straight and stared at her in surprise, his eyes at half-mast, his hair standing on end. The quilt fell away, revealing a bare, bronzed chest. It caused her to wonder what they wore or didn't wear up there in the land of the midnight sun. She turned away, not knowing what else he wasn't wearing and afraid to find out.

"Come back here," he said with a low chuckle. "I want my breakfast. In bed."

She looked over her shoulder to find him grinning at her, the blankets just barely covering the lower half of his body so that she still didn't know what, if anything, he was wearing under there.

"In bed?" she croaked, more disturbed than she'd admit by the sight of a half-naked man in her upstairs bedroom. A sight she might have to get used to if she had any more single guests.

"It says in the brochure..." he reminded her.

"I know." Those words were beginning to be the bane of her existence. She turned to the door and gripped the handle for support. "What would you like?"

There was a long pause. "Whatever you're offering."

She looked over her shoulder again. She couldn't help it, she had to see the expression on his face. What she saw was the grin that set her nerves tingling, that made her feel more alive than a spray of ocean salt water on her skin. She swallowed hard. "You're easy," she remarked.

"That's the first nice thing you've said to me," he said.

"Really?" She searched her mind. If she hadn't said anything nice, she'd certainly thought it. She'd thought about him far into the night, about how he looked across the table or across the room, about how his lips had felt on hers and how wrong it was to want more. She'd concluded about three in the morning that, once he got over his fear of commitment and his belief that all women were as shallow as his first wife, he would be perfect for someone. But not her. She wasn't perfect for anybody. If she was, she'd be married by now. At thirty-two, she'd come to terms with her limitations. And she should know by now that some men just liked to flirt. Take Adam, for example, oozing sex appeal from his bed. It took all of her willpower to open the door and march down the stairs to cook breakfast for him.

By the time she returned, he'd probably be dressed. He'd better be dressed. There was just so much a warm-blooded woman could take. She hadn't known how susceptible she was. She'd thought that writing letters to some faraway man was a substitute for a real, living, breathing hunk of masculinity, but last night she'd learned that it wasn't. She'd learned she had needs that couldn't be fulfilled by long distance.

She knew it would never happen again—someone appearing at her doorstep, cooking her dinner, entertaining her guests and looking at her as if she were good enough to eat.

Not only did men like Adam never come alone to a bed and breakfast, no men usually came at all. For her sake, however, she hoped this wasn't the end.

In the kitchen, she brewed a fresh pot of Guatemalan coffee, poached a perfect egg, nestled it on top of a toasted English muffin and drenched it all in hollandaise sauce. She framed the dish with homemade pork sausages and added a glass of fresh-squeezed juice before she started up the stairs. Knocking lightly on the door, she felt a tremor of breathless anticipation charge through her body. If he didn't answer soon she'd have hollandaise all over the mini-apron that partly covered her camp shirt and freshly laundered jeans.

"Come in," he called, but she didn't have a free hand to open the door.

"I, uh, I can't..."

The door swung open and he stood there in plaid boxers, as nonchalant as if he was at the Hilton and she was room service. She tore her eyes away from his strapping frame and took a deep breath.

"You still... you still want it in bed?" she asked.

His eyes gleamed. "All of it." He made a flying leap onto the bed, pulled the striped sheet up to his waist and eyed her expectantly.

She concentrated on unfolding the wooden tray legs so she wouldn't have to meet his blatantly sexy gaze. He seemed to enjoy having her here in his bedroom. Or was it just the novelty of having breakfast in bed? Walking to the bed, she fit the tray legs around his thighs, her fingers brushing the sheet. Then she pulled back and knotted her hands behind her.

How could she be in the bed-and-breakfast business if she couldn't serve breakfast to a guest without coming apart at the seams? Her face felt flushed and her breath came in short bursts. She backed toward the door as fast as she could.

"Sit down," he instructed, inhaling the steam from the coffee. "I hate to eat alone." He gestured toward the foot of his bed.

Mandy stared at his bed as if she'd never seen it before. She pictured herself perched on the edge, feeling the vibrations from his body. Deliberately she walked to the window seat and sat down on the flat cushion. After all, he was a guest. And if guests hated to eat alone...

He cut himself a large piece of the egg and muffin with its accompanying sauce and closed his eyes to savor the combination of flavors. "You made this?" he asked.

"Yes."

"What else can you make?"

"Breakfasts, that's all."

"That's enough," he said, cutting a sausage into pieces. "We'd make a great team, you and I. I do dinners, you do breakfasts. If you're interested in teaming up, that is." He looked at her over his coffee cup.

"I'm not and neither are you," she reminded him.

"Oh, that's right," he said, staring at her, noticing the way she was outlined against the window, her glorious hair that he wanted to plow his hands through, her firm, upturned breasts under her crisp shirt. Not to mention the apron that just barely covered her thighs.

Ever since she'd appeared in the doorway looking like a French maid in Levi's, he'd fantasized about untying that little apron from around her waist and taking her to bed with him. He rubbed his free hand over his forehead and reminded himself of why he was there. To get to know Mandy—but not in the physical sense. He drained his coffee cup.

"What are we going to do today?" he asked.

"*We?*"

"It says in the brochure..." he began, holding it up as evidence.

"I know what it says, I wrote it myself."

"I thought so. It sounds like you, warm and kind and caring. So caring you wouldn't leave a guest on his own, would you?"

"Well, what *would* you want to do?" She crossed the room and stood at the door, looking apprehensive.

There were so many things he wanted to do, it made his head swim. And they all began with removing that little apron and went on from there. It wasn't easy seeing her stand so close, her skin suffused with a faint flush, and think about sight-seeing when all the sights he wanted to see were right in this room.

"There are so many possibilities," he said, trying to focus on the brochure in his hands. "So much to choose from. There are the tide pools, the Winchester Mystery House, the elephant seals and...whatever else you suggest." Lifting the tray aside and placing it on the floor by the bed, he stood and stretched, and she turned toward the door. "So if you want to get ready, I'll change and meet you downstairs in a half hour or so."

She shot him a look over her shoulder that told him what he wanted to know. She was not yet bewitched, but she was definitely bothered and bewildered. And Jack had nothing to do with it. That shouldn't make Adam feel so smug and self-satisfied. It shouldn't make him look forward to a day alone with Mandy, either, so much so that his heart pounded with anticipation, but it did, and he was. But as long as he kept his feelings to himself and acted like a casual guest, where was the harm?

Mandy threw a load of clothes into the washing machine, the dishes in the dishwasher, made up the beds the Davises had occupied, and finally outlined her lips with gloss and grabbed a sweater. October days along the coast were usually warm, but evenings could be chilly. Evenings? Who said anything about evenings? She was going out to show Adam the sights. A brief outing where she would give an overall view of the surroundings so he could find his own way around for the rest of his stay. She hadn't been in this business very long, but she didn't think that most hostesses actually accompanied their guests on tours of the area. For one thing, they were too busy. Why wasn't she? Good question. She must be doing something wrong.

Adam was sitting in the front parlor when she came in from her bedroom. He was wearing khaki pants and a blue polo shirt that didn't hide the muscles in his arms, muscles acquired not from lifting weights at a health club, but from drilling for oil in the Arctic Sea. She tore her gaze away and looked at the reading material in his hands.

He raised his arms, held out his palms and the brochures scattered over the floor. "I want to see it all. Where do we start?"

She smiled at his enthusiasm. "I don't know," she admitted. "I haven't been to most of these places, either. You know how it is when you live someplace. You take things for granted. I don't get out much." That was putting it mildly. She didn't get out at all. She'd buried herself in her house, telling herself she had too much work to do. The truth was, she had no one to do things with. Even when her sister was home, she was never really home.

Mandy leaned down and picked up a folder from the floor. There was a picture of a giant, award-winning pumpkin, grown right down the road in Half Moon Bay, self-proclaimed pumpkin capital of the world. "Good grief," she said, "it's almost Halloween. We can hit the pumpkin festival on our way down the coast."

Adam rose to his feet and stood behind Mandy, looking at the picture over her shoulder, his breath warm on the back of her neck.

"Unless you...unless you'd rather do s-something else," she stammered.

The something else was becoming obvious by the brush of his lips against the sensitive spot behind her ear. "There's nothing I'd like better," he murmured in her ear, "than to take you—" he paused and she felt his tongue trace the tender outline of her ear "—to a pumpkin festival."

Mandy felt a weakness in her limbs as if they'd suddenly turned into putty. She crumbled the folder in her hand and lurched forward. "Then let's go."

They took his rental car. Mandy gave directions while she silently reminded herself that she was out on a fact-finding mission so she could be better informed about the attractions of the area. The problem was that the attractions of Adam Gray threatened to overshadow anything the coastal area could offer, including the famous pumpkin festival. And as they drove along the coast highway with the ocean on her right and green fields of the commercial flower growers on her left, she asked herself if all this wasn't just a little too good to be true.

The best-looking, sexiest, most rugged hunk of manhood, right out of *Yukon Man* just drops into her bed and breakfast and proceeds to knock her off her feet. Things like that just didn't happen to Mandy Clayton. Not unless there was a catch. What was the catch? She slid a glance at Adam and he reached for her hand, placing it on his muscular thigh. Mandy grabbed her hand back as if she'd been burned.

"I'm afraid you've got the wrong idea about bed-and-breakfast owners," she said, staring straight ahead, her hands knotted in her lap.

"Maybe I do," he admitted freely with an amused glance. "After all, this is my first time. I've never stayed at one before. Do you mean all the hostesses aren't like you?"

She felt her face flush. "No. Yes ... I don't know. I just know that I *don't* think they flirt with their guests."

"Is that what you're doing, flirting with me? Because I'm not looking for a flirtation, Mandy," he said, his eyes darkening.

Mandy rolled down her window and let the ocean breeze cool her cheeks. "Maybe we should start all over. Define the rules. Restate the situation," she suggested, proud of how steady her voice was when she could still feel the muscles of his thigh against her palm.

"Fair enough." His tone was light. He was enjoying teasing her, seeing how far she'd go. Well, she wasn't going any further than this, not until she knew more about this mystery man. "The way I see it," he continued, making a left turn at the sign for the historic town of Half Moon Bay, "is that you're the best thing that ever happened to a bed and breakfast. You've entertained me, enlightened me and served me the most fantastic breakfast in bed I've ever had. So far," he added with a gleam in his eye she couldn't ignore, a gleam that suggested other ideas for breakfasts in bed that made her head spin. "And now," he continued, "you're showing me around. I don't know how I can pay you back, do you?"

Mandy ignored the loaded question and pointed to a parking space behind the junior high school. She was beginning to regret she'd asked him to restate the rules. No matter what she said, it led to another suggestion on his part that was loaded with double, even triple meanings that she didn't dare contemplate. Only, she *was* contemplating them, so much so that she stumbled over a brick on Main Street. He caught her hand and held it tightly as they wove through the throngs of people engaged in pumpkin-pie-eating contests, pumpkin carving and face painting.

"Want your face painted?" he asked as they watched a beautiful blue star being painted on the cheek of a little girl.

"Isn't it just for kids?" Mandy asked, aware of his warm fingers against her palm, aware that she could pull away from him but didn't.

He shook his head and when the painter finished with the child, he sat Mandy down on the stool and suggested the "princess look" with sparkles around her blue eyes and a beauty mark next to the dimple in her cheek.

She didn't need paint to look like a princess, Adam thought, watching the artist at work, but, good God, she was beautiful, with her lips red and full, her eyes highlighted with blue, glitter sprinkled over her cheeks. She looked up at him questioningly, her painted lashes making shadows on her cheeks. "Nice," he said, in the understatement of the year.

"Your turn," she said, vacating the stool.

"Oh, no," he protested. "That's kid stuff." The dimple flashed in her cheek as she placed her hands on his shoulders and firmly pushed him onto the stool in front of the artist.

"I think a pirate look would be appropriate," she told the painter, who proceeded to draw a patch around one eye and a roguish mustache above Adam's upper lip. He sent Mandy a baleful look. "Fair's fair," she told him cheerfully. But already she regretted making him look any more attractive than he already was. Not only did he look dashing, he looked downright lecherous as a pirate. They paid the artist and continued to wend their way past balloon booths, pumpkin ice cream, and T-shirts, unaware of the admiring glances of passersby.

"I must look ridiculous," he muttered as three teenage girls giggled and swiveled their heads in his direction.

"You don't look ridiculous," she assured him. "You look...dangerous."

He stopped in the middle of the blocked-off street, oblivious to the people who milled around them. "I'm not dangerous," he said, allowing the crowd to push him so close to her he could see the flecks of green in her blue eyes. "I'm hungry," he said. And before she could answer, his lips were on hers, quick and urgent and hungry, while the throngs milled around him. He kissed her once and then again and again until she was breathless and weak in the knees. Dazed, she pulled back and looked around, but no one noticed them. No one cared that a one-eyed pirate and a princess were locked in a passionate embrace on Main Street. No one but Adam, who looked a little dazed himself and more than a little self-satisfied.

"I've been wanting to do that since I got here," he said.

Mandy took a deep breath. "If you're still hungry," she suggested, "we could pick up some fish and chips down by the water." Adam grinned at her, took her hand and they walked down to the breakwater to buy their food and eat on top of the rocks.

Adam felt the spray from the waves smashing against the rocks below, and watched Mandy out of the corner of his eye. It was a good thing Jack hadn't happened along Main Street that morning, Adam thought, a wave of guilt threatening him more than the waves below. Jack wouldn't want Adam to go this far in his research. Her kissing ability was not in question. If it was, he'd have to recommend Mandy for her soft lips and the promise of passion just lurking below the surface.

Jack would definitely not approve of the turn the investigation was taking. Adam knew that, and yet he couldn't seem to stop. The more he discovered what Mandy was like, the more he desired her. Yes, he had to admit it, she'd exceeded his expectations. He knew from her letters she was bright and funny, but he hadn't known she was sexy as hell. But he had a duty to leave her alone because she wasn't his and never would be. She belonged to Jack, or so Jack thought. What did Mandy think?

He leaned back against a boulder and looked out to the horizon. "You said you weren't married," he began.

She threw a handful of crumbs to the sea gulls who hovered overhead, waiting for a handout. "So?" she inquired, tilting her head in his direction.

"So I was wondering if there's anyone special, anyone I should know about..." He trailed off. It would serve him right if she told him it was none of his business. "Never mind," he said abruptly. "It's none of my business." He didn't want to hear her say, "Yes, there's this guy in the Yukon, the one I mentioned, sensitive, kind, honest. His name is Jack Larue." He didn't want to hear about Jack. But he had to think about him. Jack was his best friend and this was the woman his best friend was going to marry. Maybe.

Mandy stood and held out her hand to him. He took it and pulled himself up next to her. "Sometimes," she said, drawing her eyebrows together, "I don't understand you."

"Sometimes I don't understand myself," he admitted, brushing a crumb off the corner of her mouth. A cloud of glitter from her cheek dusted his hand. Was that all he was going to get out of this deal? While Jack got the gold, he got the glitter? Well, what did he expect, that Mandy would fall into his arms and throw away the opportunity to marry a millionaire? Not a chance. She was still looking at him, her blue eyes wide and expectant, waiting for him to make the next move.

"We'd better head back," he said gruffly.

Startled, her eyes widened and he hated himself for bringing their day to an abrupt halt. But it was better to do it now than later. Because sooner or later she'd find out who he was and she'd hate him for lying to her.

"Of course," she said stiffly, pulling her hand from his. "I've got work to do. And who knows, maybe some more guests?" She forced a cheerful smile and led the way back to the car, along the sand and around the edge of town and back to the street. Stuck on the windshield of the rented Toyota was a flyer for the Winchester Mystery House's flashlight tour. A Halloween Special.

"Ever been there?" Adam asked, opening the car door for her.

"Not, but I know the story. Mrs. Winchester was the heiress to the Winchester rifle fortune. She believed she'd die if she ever quit building on to her house. The rooms go on and on. They say they're haunted..."

"Afraid to go there?" he asked.

"Of course not. Are you?"

He backed the car out of the lot. "I'm not afraid of anything." *Except women,* he wanted to say. *I'm afraid of getting involved with them, afraid of hurting and getting hurt. Afraid of* you, *Mandy, especially you.* "Except the dark," he added with a smile. "I'm afraid of being alone in the dark."

He felt her eyes on him. "You wouldn't be alone. I'd be with you."

"That's what I'm afraid of," he confessed. He wasn't sure he could handle any more aloneness with Mandy, especially in the dark. Not in his present capacity as friend of the groom. "Anyway, I've got to get back and make some calls, okay?"

"Of course." Mandy's head was swimming. She could have sworn he was going to take her to the haunted house, and for some strange reason she had wanted to go, to hold his hand as they stumbled in the dark from room to room. But here they were on their way home already. How could

she have misunderstood? Unless Adam was deliberately
leading her on . . . Maybe he couldn't help it. Maybe he was
subject to violent mood swings caused by all those seismic
blasts he'd experienced in the Yukon.

Jack, on the other hand, was as steady as a rock. She
folded her arms across her seat belt. Maybe every other man
would look flaky next to Jack. Maybe Jack wasn't as good-
looking as Adam—no one was—but give her a dependable,
down-to-earth guy any day. One who would keep his word,
who wouldn't promise what he couldn't deliver, who was
interested in making a commitment. Who was, in fact, actively pursuing marriage as a goal. *That* was what she was
looking for. Wasn't it strange she'd found him in the pages
of *Yukon Man*?

Chapter Four

Adam parked the car in the circular drive in front of the Miramar Inn, and Mandy jumped out and reached her hand into the steel gray mailbox. She drew out a batch of bills and one long blue airmail envelope that was postmarked the Yukon. Her heart skipped a beat. She fumbled for her keys until Adam took them out of her hand and unlocked the front door. She looked up to thank him, but he wasn't looking at her, he was staring at the letter in her hand.

"I recognize the stamps," he explained, his brow furrowed. "Would that be from your friend, Jack What's-his-name?"

"Larue," she said absently, tossing her purse in the direction of her desk, then sinking onto the couch and ripping open the envelope. She glanced up. Adam was standing in the middle of the room looking down at her intently. Holding the blue stationery tightly between her fingers, she paused.

She didn't want company while she read Jack's letter. Not even Adam. *Especially* not Adam. He wasn't one of those people you could ignore. When he was around, you knew it. They exchanged a long glance.

"Yes?" she said finally.

"Aren't you going to check your answering machine?" he asked.

"I'm going to read my letter first," she said firmly.

"Okay." He took the chair opposite her, across from the fireplace. "I'll just hang out for a while."

Mandy frowned at him, annoyed at the way he'd settled in as if he were there to stay. Just when she wanted to be alone. Alone with Jack's letter. She could go into her room, of course, but she always read Jack's letters here in the living room where she could imagine sharing a glass of wine with him in front of a blazing fire. She knew it was silly. He'd never said anything about coming down to see her, but he'd often said he didn't want to spend his life in the Yukon. Unlike Adam, who wanted to get farther away from people, Jack was so gregarious, so outgoing. Too outgoing to spend his life in the frozen North with only bears for company.

She tucked her legs under her and tried to ignore the presence of the man seated across from her. "Dear Mandy," the letter began. "The nights grow long now that it's October—"

"Good news?" Adam interrupted.

She glared at him. "I'm only on the first sentence...do you mind?"

"Mind? Of course not. Go ahead."

"Thank you." Mandy sank farther into the recesses of the couch, finally able to put aside the memory of Adam and the pumpkin festival until he spoke again.

"Is there anything you want me to explain, any expressions you don't understand?" he inquired, getting to his feet and standing in front of the fireplace.

Mandy tore her eyes reluctantly from her letter and looked up at him. "No. Thank you. He speaks English, you know. Almost as well as you do."

Adam pressed his lips together and nodded thoughtfully. "Glad to hear it. I just thought there might be some Canadian slang or something I could help you with."

"He doesn't use slang," she explained very carefully. In about one minute she was going to tell Adam to either leave the room or shut up. Though it wasn't really recommended that hostesses tell their guests to shut up or go to their room, she'd reached the end of her rope.

"What does he use?" Adam asked, bracing one elbow against the mantel.

Mandy rubbed her hands and a shower of glitter landed in her lap. "I think I'll take a shower," she said in a tone of resignation. "You're right, this stuff gets all over everything."

He nodded. "I told you."

She sailed past him, sweater in one hand, the letter in the other, went into her bedroom and closed the door firmly behind her. She tossed her sweater onto the chair and the letter into the middle of her queen-size bed, then stripped her clothes off and entered the bathroom. She turned on the shower. Adam was the strangest person she'd ever met. Sometimes he seemed eager to get away from her, other times, like just now, he wouldn't leave her alone for a minute. Maybe everyone who went to the Yukon was peculiar in some way? Everyone but Jack, that is. Either they went to the Yukon because they were unusual, or they became that way after they'd been there awhile.

Above the noise of the shower, she heard someone knocking on her door and calling her name. She turned the spigot off and wrapped a towel around her. At her bedroom door, she paused. "Yes?"

"Mandy," Adam said. "Telephone."

She opened the door and he handed her the portable phone. He'd changed. He'd showered. He looked clean and gorgeous, his dark hair damp and thick. She gripped her towel tightly around her chest with her other hand. "Thank you."

He nodded. "Wait a minute. You missed a few places." He took a clean white handkerchief out of his pocket and ran it over her cheek to remove the last traces of face paint. His touch was so unexpected, so intimate, that she shivered. Then he used the square of white cotton to blot her lips. She trembled. She tried to tell him to stop, but she couldn't speak. She tried to back away into her room, but she couldn't make her legs work. So she closed her eyes and gave in to the delicious sensations leaping from her lips to her brain and back again. The next thing she knew he was trailing his lips to the hollow of her neck, where her pulse throbbed.

She gave a ragged sigh, oblivious to the telephone receiver she was still clutching with one hand. When he ran one finger along the top of her towel, her eyes flew open and she saw he was looking at her with a devilish grin. "It's your sister," he said with a glance at the telephone. "Tell her I said hello." And with that he closed the door behind him.

Mandy stumbled backward onto her bed and landed on her back, breathing hard.

"It's about time," Laurie complained. "Where were you, upstairs? You're panting."

Mandy took a deep breath. "No, I'm not."

"Who answered the phone?"

"A guest."

"Is he as sexy as he sounds?"

Mandy flopped over on her stomach and buried her face in the quilt. If Laurie only knew, she'd fly home immediately. Which was not a good idea. She would throw herself at Adam or she would throw Mandy at him. Either way would be a disaster.

Mandy raised her head and got her breathing under control. "So-so," she said at last.

"Is he there with his wife or anything?"

"He has no wife. I don't know about the anything. Probably not, since he lives in the Yukon." Mandy bit her lip and changed the subject. "How was your flight?" she asked.

"The Yukon?" Laurie asked, ignoring her question. "Isn't that a coincidence?"

"Not really. I advertise in *Yukon Man*, remember? At your suggestion, I might add. That's where he read about the inn."

"So it's just the two of you alone in the house?" Laurie continued.

"Not at all. In fact, I was full last night."

"And tonight?"

"Well, I..."

It may have been fate, or maybe providence, but at that moment there was another knock on her bedroom door.

"Mandy, come on out. There are some people here looking for a room."

"Did you hear that?" Mandy asked Laurie. "More guests. Talk to you later." Mandy threw on her hostess outfit again, ran a comb through her wet hair, left her face the way it was, and hurried into the living room.

There was Adam leaning against the fireplace mantel in a navy blue sweater and gray slacks as if he belonged there, entertaining a young couple with some story about an oil strike in the Middle East.

On second glance they didn't look entertained at all, they looked completely engrossed in each other. In fact, they scarcely looked up when Adam introduced her to them.

"Mandy, this is Jane and her, uh, Ben. They've pretty much decided to take the room. Special weekday rate I quoted them. I was just going to carry their luggage in, but they don't have any." He gave her a quizzical look, followed by a knowing grin.

"Oh, fine," Mandy gasped. "Would you like to sign the register?" she asked, turning on the lamp over the desk.

Jane tore her adoring gaze from Ben for a brief moment, but kept her arm around his waist, her hip firmly wedged against his. "Could we do it later?" she asked. "We've been on the road for hours and we're anxious to relax. Your husband was just going to show us the room." Jane and her companion exchanged a long, hungry look that sizzled with so much sexual tension that Mandy had to look away. She meant to say that Adam wasn't her husband, but she didn't think they really cared. By the time she looked up again, Adam was halfway up the stairs with Jane and Ben following close behind. And in another minute he was back in the living room.

"I'd say they got here just in the nick of time," Adam said, rubbing his hands together.

"Do you think they're married?" Mandy asked.

"No, but they think we are."

Mandy blushed. "It's a common mistake."

"Amen," Adam said with a wry twist of his lips.

"Was it that bad?" Mandy asked, perching on the arm of the chair.

"I wouldn't recommend it. It's a sure way to ruin a relationship. Take Jane and Ben there." He glanced toward the staircase, listening to the muffled laughter from somewhere upstairs. "If they were married, they'd be sitting here talk-

ing to us over sherry, and stuffing themselves with your delicious hors d'oeuvres, instead of... you know.''

"I know," she said quickly, feeling her cheeks flush.
"Fortunately for the propagation of the human race," she
added, "not everyone feels the way you do about marriage
and children. Some men are actively looking for someone to
marry."

"So I've heard," he said. "They even advertise in mag-
azines."

She straightened her shoulders. "Maybe they have to
if they live in the Yukon—a zillion miles from nowhere.
Maybe they have no choice."

Adam didn't like the defensive tone in her voice. Because
he knew who she was defending. It was Jack. Jack, who sat
up there in the land of the midnight sun, surrounded by
stacks of letters and pictures of beautiful women who sent
homemade cakes and cookies from as far away as Florida
and Vermont. Jack, who could have chosen anyone, who
had chosen Mandy and Julie from Illinois. With a little help
from Adam.

Yes, he was partly to blame for Jack's interest in Mandy.
And Mandy's interest in Jack, after all, he'd written his
share of the letters. But he hadn't written the one she'd
gotten today. The one he'd last seen lying in the middle
of her bed. What was in it? Had Jack decided on Mandy?
Would Jack decide without telling Adam? Without Adam's
steadying influence, Jack might make a snap decision he'd
regret. Which made it imperative for Adam to get in touch
with Jack right now and find out what the hell was going on.

"Do you mind if I make a call before we go out to dinner?"

"Of course not... what?"

"The Seadrift sounds good to me, unless you have somewhere else in mind."

"Oh, I don't think..."

"You don't think it would be any fun for me to eat by myself and I appreciate that." He left the mantel, crossed the room and put his hands on her shoulders. "You know I hate to eat by myself."

It was a lie. He'd eaten alone for years. In the Yukon they often worked shifts and never saw anybody at mealtime. On the other hand, that was before he'd met Mandy. Before yesterday. Before he'd shared dinner with her in her kitchen, breakfast in his bedroom and lunch on the breakwater. He had a sudden desire to eat every meal with her from now on to see if he could outdo the one before. Which was going to be a little difficult since she might very likely marry Jack and Jack might not appreciate Adam showing up for dinner every night. She was looking up at him with such a guileless, trusting look in her blue eyes he had to look away, over her shoulder and out the window. But he kept his hands on her shoulders.

"Anyway," he continued, "we can't hang around here and think about what they're doing upstairs. And you're all dressed up with no place to go." He let his hands slide down her arms, feeling the warmth of her skin under the soft knit sweater, aware of the smell of soap that clung to her skin. Unable to shake the vision of her in her room with her towel knotted above her breasts, he finally pulled away. "Back in a flash," he promised. "Can I use the phone in the kitchen?"

He didn't wait for her answer. He made a dash for the kitchen while he could still function. Adam dialed the number and Jack answered on the third ring.

"I've been trying to call you all day. Where have you been?" Jack demanded.

"Out."

"Where was Mandy?"

"She was out, too. What's up, have you made the big decision?"

"I can't until I get some input from you. I'm sitting here waiting to hear from you and you're 'out.'" Jack sounded definitely steamed.

"Do you think I want to be out? Do you think I enjoy doing your undercover work for you? You don't think I'm having a good time, do you?" Adam demanded just a shade too sharply.

"That's exactly what I think. I haven't heard from you all day. And when I do talk to you all I get is 'she's nice.' Is it too much to ask for more information? A few details?"

Adam straddled the kitchen chair and tried to think. What to say about Mandy? "She's a good cook," he admitted finally.

"Really? She runs a bed and breakfast and she's a good cook. That's great." Sarcasm dripped from Jack's voice. "Give me a break."

"You know what?" Adam said. "You're not yourself today. You need a vacation."

"I don't need a vacation. I need a wife," Jack snapped. "That's what this is all about. Or have you forgotten?"

"I haven't forgotten. And that reminds me. Mandy has never been married, but she's been hurt, and hurt badly. So go easy. You can't come on too strong. What did you say in your letter? I thought I was handling the letters to Mandy."

"I decided to take over. Especially since you're not here. I can't expect you to keep writing to her when you're under the same roof. What did she say about my letter?" Jack asked.

"Nothing. What did you say in your letter?"

"Nothing. None of your business."

"Wait a minute. I thought this *was* my business. What happened to Julie?"

"She's on hold. But she doesn't like being on hold. She just sent me a scarf she knitted herself."

"Well, wrap it around your neck and go for a hike. It'll do you good to get out."

"Don't tell me what will do me good. The only advice I want from you is whether I should propose to Mandy or not. Would I be happy married to Mandy?"

"Probably. But would Mandy be happy married to you? Especially when she finds out you're not a millionaire."

"I'm a potential millionaire. All I need is one lucky strike. There's a new gold rush on, you know. Just since you left three guys have staked a claim at Granger's Camp. There's gold in the air, I can smell it. So just find out if Mandy's interested in the money or me."

"Okay, okay. I'll see what I can do. But I have to take her out to dinner to find out that kind of thing."

"Is that absolutely necessary?"

"Absolutely. This is a delicate operation. You don't expect me to take her to some local bar and buy her a few beers, do you? I didn't think so. I've gotta run now. Talk to you later."

"Wait a minute," Jack shouted. "How much later? Call me when you get back from dinner."

Adam put the phone back in the receiver without answering. He'd be damned if he'd call Jack after every conversation with Mandy. Or after every meal. He hurried back to the living room. With one last glance at the stairway, where their guests had last been seen, Adam hustled Mandy out the front door and into his car. They were at the Seadrift a few minutes later.

Adam let his eyes drift over the top of his menu to drink in the sight of Mandy across the table. Mandy interested in money? Mandy a gold digger? It wasn't possible, was it? He cleared his throat. "How do you feel about money, Mandy?"

"I like it," she said with a smile. "Don't you?"

"I like what it buys," he admitted. "Good food, good wine and a good vacation in California every once in a while."

"I'll drink to that," Mandy said, raising her glass of a light California Chenin Blanc. "If only there were more of you, I wouldn't have to worry so much."

"What do you worry about?" he asked, setting his menu on the table.

"The usual. Paying the bills. It's a risky business, bed and breakfasts. Most of them go belly-up within the first year. The only reason I've been able to hold on is because Laurie pays me rent. But I could sure use a big infusion of cash to make some improvements, advertise more..."

When the waiter came, they ordered oysters on the half shell, shrimp scampi with wild rice, and a Caesar salad for two.

"What about you?" Mandy asked, folding her hands on the tablecloth. "What do you worry about, Adam?"

He wanted to say he worried she'd fallen in love with a man who didn't exist. A millionaire who had Jack's goals but Adam's personality. He worried about Jack's finding the right woman; he worried about Mandy finding out that Jack had lied to her. But most of all, he worried about what was happening to him, getting involved with Mandy despite his best intentions.

The way she looked at him, her blue eyes the color of the sea at dusk, made him want to confess everything, get it all out at once, clear the air and tell the truth. But it was too late. He was in too deep and Jack had too much to lose.

"What, me worry?" he asked with a grin. "I'm on vacation. I've got no worries at all." Then he remembered his mission. "So you could use some extra money, couldn't you?"

"Of course, couldn't everyone?" She took a bite of salad and chewed thoughtfully.

"Tell me about your friend Jack, maybe I've run into him somewhere," Adam said.

"I thought you said it was a big territory."

"It is," he assured her. "But there aren't many people up there. How did you meet in the first place?"

Mandy squirmed uncomfortably. She would never, ever, admit to anyone in a thousand years that she'd answered a personal ad. And she would never, ever, admit to herself that Jack was anything more than just a pen pal. Only she knew that her heart beat a little faster every time she got a letter from him. Only she was aware of how much she looked forward to those letters.

"It's a long story," she said at last. "Actually, we're just pen pals."

"You mean, you've never met him?"

"How could I? He lives in the Yukon, a zillion miles from nowhere. But I know him better than most people I actually know," she said stiffly.

"You don't know what he looks like?" Adam asked.

"It's not important. He's just a friend."

"A special friend, though," Adam insisted, leaning forward and tilting her chin up with his thumb.

She met his gaze as her knees brushed his under the table and there it was again, that electricity in the air, the sparks flying between them. Even as they were discussing Jack, Adam was causing sparks to fly through the air. Then he pulled back sharply, almost as if he'd received an electric shock, too.

Mandy scooted back in her chair and refolded her napkin in her lap. "A very special friend," she repeated. "By that I mean that Jack is not an ordinary oil rigger. He writes the most beautiful letters. Maybe it's the solitude that brings out the sensitivity in some men."

"Solitude?" Adam asked, gripping his wineglass in his hand. "Doesn't he have a roommate or anything?"

"Oh, yes, I guess so. But they have nothing in common. Jack never mentions him. He's probably just an ordinary guy."

"Probably," Adam said ruefully. "And you can tell about all this sensitivity from his letters?"

"You're so skeptical," Mandy remarked, savoring the sauce on her shrimp. "But you wouldn't be if you actually knew Jack. You might even like him if you met him."

"What about you?" Adam asked, studying the way her hair brushed her shoulders. "You're the one who should meet him. That's the only way to find out . . ."

She looked up from her wild rice. "Find out what?"

"If you want to take the next step, move from friendship to something else."

"I already know. I was in love once. It was the most painful experience of my life."

"So your sister's right. You *are* afraid to get involved, to make a commitment."

She straightened her spine against the back of the chair. "What about you, hiding out on a drilling platform? Talk about fear of commitment."

He held up his hand. "Guilty as charged. Twenty-foot waves I can take. Gale-force winds and minus zero temperatures. But women are ten times as dangerous. When my wife left, I couldn't get out of bed in the mornings. I felt like I'd been hit over the head with a piece of drill pipe. I'd rather be swept out to sea by a giant wave than go through that again. No more women in my life. Never."

Mandy felt as if *she'd* been hit by a ten-foot wave herself, so firm was his voice, so vehement his argument. She held up her hand to protect herself from the force of his words. "You don't have to convince me," she said. "I understand exactly what you mean. I mean, if we can't learn from our mistakes, what's the use of living? I've never been happier being on my own, making my own way in the world." Her blue eyes shot sparks into the air, so bright he wanted to shield his eyes. There was no doubting her sincerity, Adam thought, and yet . . .

"Me, either," he countered, and took her hand in his. "Let's shake on it." But instead of shaking her hand, he just held it for a long moment. He didn't mean to. But for some reason he couldn't let go. He couldn't break the connection, the bond they'd formed in just the short time they'd known each other.

It was getting harder and harder to keep Jack in mind. To keep his interests first and foremost. Even though they seemed to talk about him nonstop, even though she obviously thought about him and treasured his letters, Adam didn't want to think about him at all. Not with Mandy sitting across the table from him, her hair a soft cloud around her face, her hand in his, her knees just a whisper away, so close he could brush them by accident any time he moved.

And then he felt it, like the ten-foot wave he'd mentioned, the kind he wasn't afraid of. A rush of envy hit him so hard his chest hurt. He wanted to be Jack, he wanted her to talk about him the way she talked about Jack, with the same breathless reverence. He wanted to be that rare combination of sensitivity and rugged Yukon man she obviously admired.

No matter what she said about not wanting to take the next step, he knew she was just protecting herself. She might not know it, but all it would take would be for Jack to show up and sweep her off her feet. Of course, there was that protective shell she'd built around herself. It would take some sensitivity to work through that. If he were Jack he'd know exactly what to do.

But he wasn't Jack. He let her hand go. He was Adam, Jack's best friend. And he was not available for a commitment the way Jack was. Jack was ready for the big M word. Marriage and children and all that. What every woman

wanted. Even Mandy. No matter what she said, it was what
she wanted.

How could he stand between her and what she wanted?
He couldn't. She and Jack deserved each other. And he'd
have to do his best to see that they got each other. When he
got back he'd call Jack and tell him the truth. Mandy was
the right woman for him, she had everything he could want.
She was sweet, kind, ambitious, hardworking, warm and
loving. But Jack had to go slow, realize what she'd been
through, show her that all men weren't the same, that some
of them could be trusted. Yes, it was clear now what his
mission was. No more confusion. No more getting carried
away by the sight of her in a wet towel, by the touch of her
lips, the look in her eyes.

"Dessert?" he asked, and she shook her head.

"Why don't we have coffee back home?" she suggested.

"Fine," he said. But it wasn't fine. He couldn't trust
himself to sit down across from her at the kitchen table, as
if he belonged there. It was Jack who belonged there, not
him. And besides, a cup of coffee could lead to something
else. "I'll have to make a phone call first," he said.

"Your partner again?"

He took out his credit card and laid it on the plastic tray
left discreetly a moment earlier by their waiter. "He needs
my advice about an important decision."

"At ten o'clock at night?" she asked, standing.

Having received his credit card and receipt, he followed
her from the dining room. "At any hour of the day or
night."

"That's quite a responsibility," she remarked, letting him
open the car door for her.

"Only until we finish this project. Then he's on his own.
In the meantime, I'm on call, twenty-four hours a day." It
was the least he could do. Jack had done a lot for him, even
saved his life one frozen Arctic night in a whiteout. Jack had

dragged him home in the snow when he'd lost consciousness. This was his chance to pay him back. And the way to pay him back was not to steal his girl.

They didn't talk on the way home. Adam ran over the reasons to leave Mandy alone and planned his conversation with Jack. When they arrived at the bed and breakfast, Adam excused himself to make the call from his room after Mandy thanked him for dinner. He chose to ignore the hurt look in her eyes as he pretended to forget her invitation for coffee. This was no time for late-night togetherness.

"What happened?" Jack demanded as soon as he heard Adam's voice.

"Mandy's the one," Adam said, his voice sounding hollow in his ears.

"Are you sure? Julie just called. She's ready to fly up here."

"Don't let her. You've got to see Mandy first. She's got everything you're looking for."

"Then why doesn't *she* fly up here?"

"She can't. She's got a business to run. Besides, she's been burned once. You've got to handle her with care. She thinks she's not interested in marriage, but she is."

"Is she interested in me?"

"Of course. You should have seen her when she got your letter." Adam felt a pain in his chest just thinking about it.

"She liked it?"

"What did you say?"

"That's between me and her."

"If you want my advice, you'll come down here right away. But you've got to handle Mandy with care. She's different. She's vulnerable. Plan to spend some time with her. She's worth it."

"How can you be sure? You've only been there two days."

Jack was right. How did he know after only two days?
"Just a feeling."

"I'd like to come down there, but I can't leave until you
get back. Can't you hurry things up? Tell Gene you need to
see him right away, get things settled about your future and
come back to relieve me just temporarily."

"I'd like to, but Gene's busy until next week. Just hold
tight. And don't do anything rash."

"Same to you," Jack said, and hung up.

Adam turned the lights out and opened the windows to let
the sea air blow in. He stuck his head out the window as if
the air would clear his head so he'd know if he was doing the
right thing or not. He asked himself how things had gotten
so complicated. All he'd wanted to do was help Jack find a
wife. He deserved one. Someone special. But did he deserve Mandy?

He might have said no if he hadn't seen the look on her
face when she talked about Jack, the way she'd looked when
she'd gotten his letter. Would Mandy mind when she found
out Jack wasn't a millionaire? Probably not. Jack was a nice
guy with or without money. He'd realize that Mandy needed
to be cultivated, like a bruised flower bulb. A flower that
could bloom with the right amount of TLC, water and sunshine. All she needed was someone to love her and she'd
open up like a rosebud in the warm summer air. The image
he conjured up tore into him like a flat-bladed knife. What
right did Jack have to be the one to teach Mandy to love
again?

Adam lay back on the bed and crossed his arms under his
head. He reminded himself that Jack had every right to
Mandy. *He* was the one who had advertised and Mandy had
answered his ad. Whatever happened, she couldn't—
mustn't—get hurt again. The next man she fell in love with
had to come through for her. It had to be someone who had

no reservations about making a commitment. In other words, it had to be Jack.

Adam jumped up from the bed and paced around the room, studied the paintings on the wall, seascapes all of them, then chose several books from the shelves and looked them over without seeing them. Maybe he should leave right now. He'd done what he came to do and his job was finished. What was the point in staying around, torturing himself? Because it *was* torture to be so close to her and know he couldn't have her.

He couldn't have anybody. He didn't want anybody. He wanted just what he had always said he wanted. Adventure, danger and excitement. He did not want a woman to mess up his life again. If he thought he wanted Mandy, he was mistaken. He had to admit she'd thrown him off balance, but that was because he'd been in the Yukon too long doing the same job with the same partner. It was time to move on. As soon as he did, everything would be fine. He wouldn't feel restless, anxious, on edge, or suffer from insomnia.

He stared out the window until the first rays of the sun lit the ocean below, then he went downstairs and made himself a cup of coffee in Mandy's kitchen. Then he would go. He would leave her a note. He wouldn't say goodbye. Because then he might change his mind. He didn't want to see her again, not with her hair in a tangle, her long, bare legs in shorts, especially not in her hand-knit, rose-covered sweater. He didn't want to see her in anything at all. He would check in at some motel in Menlo Park and wait for Gene to show up, get his assignment, then relieve Jack so he could come down here before Adam reported to the drilling rig.

The phone rang. He let it ring twice, then he picked it up. Who would call at six in the morning? It was a travel agent from New York wanting to book both rooms for that night for some clients. Adam went to the desk in the living room and found Mandy's calendar. There were no reservations for that night or any night. Adam said okay. The agent wanted to know if the guests could have dinner there. They'd be arriving late and didn't want to go out again. Could someone pick them up at the airport?

Adam said yes and yes. Mandy needed the business. But she would need help to handle it—she didn't do dinners, so he would have to help her. It was the least he could do before he left for good, to help her get her business off the ground. Maybe the same agent would send other people. It could be the beginning.

The beginning for Mandy. The end for him. It would be a way of bowing out gracefully, with a clear conscience. More polite than leaving a note and driving off into the sunrise, anyway. He wanted her to remember him fondly if at all. Maybe she and Jack would talk about him from time to time, when they reminisced about how they met. He frowned at the calendar as he wrote down the names of the guests and their flight number. He would be on his rig and Mandy and Jack would be having coffee on the patio in the afternoons as the sun slowly sank into the ocean....

He heard the sound of footsteps on the stairs and whispers from the landing. Looking up, he saw Ben and Jane, last night's guests, coming down the stairs on tiptoe, arm in arm, pausing to exchange a soul-searching kiss, then continuing down a few more steps. They looked surprised to see Adam, gave him a check for the night and went out the front door without a backward glance.

Adam walked softly in his stocking feet to Mandy's door and listened. Not a sound. Unlike him, she was sleeping soundly. She wasn't worried about Jack. Why should she? She'd probably fallen asleep with his letter under her pillow, dreaming of him, while Adam had stared at the ceiling all night waiting for dawn. Waiting for another breakfast in bed that would never come.

Maybe it was Mandy's turn to have her breakfast in bed. The only problem was that he didn't do breakfasts. Maybe he ought to try. He'd surprise her. Surprise himself, too, if he could come up with something edible that looked like a breakfast.

Chapter Five

Mandy sat straight up in bed when she heard the knock on her door, clutching the sheet as tightly as possible under her chin. Her eyes widened in disbelief when the door opened and Adam came in, balancing a tray in one hand.

"Good morning," he said brightly, setting the tray on her nightstand. "Rise and shine." He crossed the room and yanked open the flowered curtains and let the sunshine come flooding into the room.

Mandy blinked, wishing she'd had more warning so she could have combed her hair, brushed her teeth and washed her face. She noted that Adam had probably done all of the above, as well as changing into jeans and a white short-sleeved polo shirt that did nothing to hide his golden tan or his well-developed muscles.

Never mind the muscles or the tan, it was morning, and by the strength of the sun that slanted across her bed-spread, it was late and she had to make breakfast for her guests. One of whom had apparently made it for her. She threw the covers back and swung her legs over the edge of the bed. One strap of her pale green lacy nightgown slipped over her shoulder, reminding her that she was hardly dressed for company.

"Good grief, what time must it be?" she croaked, hiking the strap back into place. "I've got to fix breakfast."

"No, you don't. The other guests left and I had my coffee in the kitchen. Of course, if you want to share those croissants I just heated up in your microwave oven..." Adam sat down on the edge of her bed and gave her a winning smile, allowing his gaze to travel over the lace that partially covered her breasts for just a brief moment before he jerked his gaze back to her face.

"You m-mean—" she stammered, pulling her legs back under the sheet and sinking down onto her pillow.

"I mean, I made your breakfast for you, just so you could see how it feels, maybe give you some ideas..."

Ideas? The ideas it gave her made her feel shivery and burning hot at the same time. She could smell the light citrus of his after-shave, and feel the weight of his body against her mattress. If he moved just half an inch toward her, or leaned in her direction, she might be tempted to forget all about breakfast. But he didn't. He stood, lifted the tray from the nightstand, and smiled at her.

"Eat up," he instructed. "You're going to need your strength when you hear the news."

The croissants were still warm and the coffee smelled so wonderful she forgot about her nightgown and sat up again as he placed the tray across her lap. The touch of his fingers against her thighs made her gasp, but he pulled away, apparently unaware of her reaction. She took a large bite of a flaky croissant.

"News?" she inquired, brushing a crumb from the corner of her mouth.

"You've got guests coming tonight. All the way from New York. They called this morning at six o'clock, nine o'clock their time. I said it was okay."

"Okay? It's wonderful! How many did you say?"

"Four. You'll be full again. I guess that means you'll need my room, too."

Mandy felt a sinking sensation in the pit of her stomach. She wasn't ready to see Adam go, even if it meant filling up her inn. "You could stay in Laurie's room, over the garage," she suggested.

He shrugged. "Or the couch. But here's the catch. The two couples are arriving by plane. We have to pick them up and they're staying for dinner."

"Dinner?" Mandy set her coffee cup down with a clatter. "Didn't you tell them I don't do dinners?"

"I couldn't. Besides, I do dinners. I'll help you."

She clutched at Adam's arm with cold fingers. "I'll need more than help."

"I'll be here," he assured her, his hand closing over hers. The touch of his hand warmed hers, the look in his eyes sent ripples of excitement charging through her body. "I'll always be here," he whispered, leaning forward, only the tray and the coffee and the croissant crumbs between them.

All she could see was the firm line of his jaw, the rich, brown velvet of his eyes, and all she wanted was for him to kiss her, just once, as if he meant it. She'd wanted it since the first minute she'd laid eyes on him. Then the words sank in and she realized what he'd said.

"What do you mean?" she demanded. "You won't always be here. You're leaving for the North Sea. How could you forget?"

He shook his head with a dazed look in his dark eyes. "It's your fault," he said, bracing his arms against her headboard and trapping her between them. "When you're around I can't remember who I am or what I'm doing here."

He pushed off the headboard and sprang to his feet by the side of her bed. "But it's all coming back to me now. I'm just passing through. But sometimes I wish..." His voice drifted off and there was such longing in his eyes she sat transfixed, waiting for him to continue, but he didn't. He picked up the tray from her lap and went to stand at the door, a safe distance away. "I wish we had some time for sight-seeing," he finished, "but we'll need to pick up some groceries before the guests come."

"We could do our shopping in the Napa Valley. It would give you a chance to visit a winery, too. Would you like that?"

She thought he'd jump at the chance for an excursion, to spend the day wandering around the valley, sampling wine, but a whole gamut of emotions she didn't understand played across his face. She didn't get it. It wasn't as if she'd suggested driving to Reno for a quickie wedding at the Little Chapel of the Wayfarer. What was he afraid of? Finally, he drew a deep breath.

"Just shopping, right?"

"Right."

He nodded and took her tray to the kitchen.

An hour later Mandy was wearing a pair of white linen pants belonging to Laurie and a beige knit shirt, and they were crossing the Golden Gate Bridge, heading north toward the Napa Valley. The fog hung over the bridge, but once they broke into Marin County the air was soft and mellow, like the wines they were going to taste.

"What did you say happened to Ben and Jane?" Mandy asked, ashamed of herself for having dismissed them from her mind so easily, even while she'd automatically ripped the sheets off their bed and put on new ones.

"They melted away at six this morning, just kind of oozed their way out the door. Ain't love grand?" he mused, opening his window to let the warm air into the car.

"Isn't it about time you stopped being so bitter?" Mandy asked.

"Bitter?" He looked surprised. "I'm not bitter. I'm just realistic. Don't tell me you believe in everlasting love?"

She squirmed uncomfortably and looked out the window at the sailboats that dotted Richardson Bay. She never used to believe, but lately, as Jack's letters got warmer and friendlier and more intimate, she began to think that maybe... just maybe...

"Do you?" he prompted.

"I think it exists," she said. "Look at George Burns and Gracie Allen. She's been dead for years, but he's still faithful to her memory."

"They were a great team," he admitted, "but we can't all be Burns and Allen."

"Or Bogart and Bacall."

"Romeo and Juliet."

"Anthony and Cleopatra."

He grinned. "Okay, you made your point. I believe it exists. Can we talk about something else?"

"That's fine with me. Tell me about you. Where did you grow up, in the Yukon?"

"Texas to start with. My dad was a wildcatter. We moved on, though, and my mother hated it. She finally went back to Boston."

Mandy turned her head to look at his profile, the straight, strong nose, the lips pressed tightly together as if he were trying to keep from saying more.

"And you?" she prompted this time.

"I stayed with him. They fought about it. She wanted to take me back with her, he wanted me with him." His voice was flat.

"What did you want?" she asked, crossing her legs.

"I wanted them to stay together. But they weren't Burns and Allen. No jokes, no everlasting love."

She nodded sympathetically. She would have liked to reach for his hand, but she had the feeling he didn't want sympathy from her. What he did want was a mystery. Why was he hanging around doing nice things like breakfast in bed for her or dinner for her guests? Sometimes she thought he didn't know what *he* wanted, either.

But there was something, something simmering below the surface of their relationship that occasionally broke the surface. Like this morning, when he'd leaned over her bed and almost kissed her. She nibbled at her lower lip, remembering the sharp pang of disappointment when she realized he wasn't going to.

What was wrong with her? What was wrong with him? Was it his vagabond childhood or his failed marriage that made him so hard to understand?

"So what happened? Did you go or stay?" she asked.

"I stayed with him until he sent me east to college. He didn't want me to be a roughneck like him, said I needed to smooth off the edges. But I think it was too late."

She studied him carefully, the rough edges, the angles, the buried feelings and the raw nerves were obvious. At least, to her. It would take an exceptional woman to understand him or to satisfy him. She sighed.

He misunderstood her long look and her sigh. "I guess you think it was too late, too."

She flushed and stared at the road ahead. "Not at all. I think you turned out fine."

"Fine," he repeated. "I'll have to remember that on those dark, cold Arctic nights. She thought I turned out 'fine.' Couldn't you come up with something a little stronger?"

"All right," she agreed. "You turned out great, as strong as Schwarzenegger, bright as Einstein, tough as Stallone, funny, too, like..."

"George Burns?"

"Definitely, and considerably younger."

He caught her eye and smiled at her. Then he slowed as the road narrowed and they approached the small town of Oakville. "I don't know about you, but I'm tired and hungry," he said, pulling over to park on the main street in front of the famous Oakville Grocery. He tilted his head back against the headrest and closed his eyes.

"Wait a minute," Mandy said. "I don't know what I'm supposed to get."

He yawned. "Whatever you want, beef, mushrooms, rice..."

She nodded. "I'll get us some lunch, too, then we can have a picnic at the winery outside town." When he closed his eyes instead of answering, she hopped out of the car. She came back half an hour later and he hadn't moved an inch.

"Adam?" she said, putting the bag of food in the back seat. Shutting the door, she seated herself in the front and closed the door behind her. "Are you all right?"

He opened his eyes. "I'm fine. I didn't get a whole lot of sleep last night. I don't know how you bed and breakfasters do it."

"We're just a remarkable bunch," she agreed. "Up at dawn to make breakfast for our guests. Want me to drive?"

He leaned forward and turned the key in the ignition. "Not yet. Just point me in the right direction."

The DuChaine winery was family owned, on a hill overlooking acres of vineyards. They took the tour, tasted a Chardonnay and a French Colombard, and Mandy bought a case of Beaujolais.

Then they left their car in the parking lot and walked to a grassy knoll, where they spread out the checkered tablecloth Mandy had brought with her, along with their deli sandwiches, a bottle of wine and some mineral water.

Adam opened the wine with the corkscrew on his Swiss Army knife and offered the bottle to Mandy. "I guess we forgot to bring glasses."

She nodded and drank from the bottle. The wine was smooth and slid down her throat easily. She leaned back against the trunk of a live oak tree and gazed dreamily out across the fields.

Adam didn't need any wine. The lack of sleep and the proximity of Mandy combined to give him a natural high. But he reached for the wine anyway, and his hand accidentally grazed her breast as he took the bottle out of her hands. He thought he heard her short, quick intake of breath, imagined he felt her response right through her knit shirt. But that couldn't be. It was just an accident.

Just as it was an accident that had brought him from the frozen North to Mandy in the Golden State. Or was it fate? Whatever it was, he had to ignore the way he felt about her, had to stop staring at her, at the way her hair curled around her face, at the smattering of freckles that appeared on her nose. Had to stop wondering how it would be to have her arms wrapped around him, to feel her body respond to his.

He took a drink of wine and tasted her lips on the bottle, sweeter than any wine. He took a sandwich to have something to do besides letting his imagination run away with him. But then he sat there looking at it, without any appetite but his hunger for Mandy, for her warm mouth, her luscious ripe body. God help him, he couldn't hold out much longer.

"Aren't you hungry?" she asked softly, and something inside him snapped like a bowstring.

"Hungry?" he asked, his voice husky with desire. "Oh, God, Mandy, if you only knew..." He never knew what happened to his sandwich, or how he covered the few feet between them, whether he crawled or leapt, or maybe even lunged. But he remembered the look in her eyes before he buried his hands in her hair and kissed her. A flash of surprise, then desire flared like the Northern Lights. Her arms wound around him just as he'd imagined, and she matched him kiss for frantic kiss as he'd never imagined, not in his wildest dreams. Their tongues entwined, her mouth was warm, soft, welcoming. And somehow they were flat on the ground, arms outstretched, hand holding hand, bodies pressed against each other.

He rolled over onto his back and pulled her on top of him. Small stones and twigs dug holes through the back of his shirt but he didn't feel them. All he felt was her breasts against his chest, her hair brushing his cheek. She smelled like sunshine, she tasted like wine, and he never wanted to let her go.

He tightened his arms around her and leaned to his side, taking her with him. Suddenly they were rolling down the slope of the grassy knoll and they were breathless and laughing as they reached the bottom and landed at the foot of a wooden fence.

His head was spinning and it wasn't all because of their speedy descent into the vineyard. It was Mandy. It was her scent, her touch, and the musical sound of her laughter. When the sound of their laughter faded, there was silence, with only the whisper of the breeze in the air. They looked into each other's eyes for a long moment, lying in the grass with the sun shining on them while the suspense mounted.

Then he cupped her face in his hands and kissed her again. Just to prove to himself that the first time wasn't a fluke. That he could make it happen again, the magic and the humming in the air around them.

Mandy was intoxicated by the nearness of him, so dizzy that she couldn't stop. It was the wine and the soft autumn air, but most of all, it was Adam, the way he felt, and the way he tasted, clean and cool and fresh. She let the kiss go on and on, deepening, lengthening. She couldn't stop, wouldn't stop. He was so hard, so warm, so strong, and he fit her so well.

Every hollow and groove of his matched a curve of hers. She'd never felt this way before, never knew it could be like this. She thought she'd loved Todd, and maybe she had, but she'd never wanted him the way she wanted Adam—more than anything. Anything she couldn't have, that is.

She stared into his eyes, eyes that threatened to swallow her up, so deep and dark she could get lost in them and never find her way out. A fly buzzed around her ear and brought her back to reality. What on earth was she doing lying here on the ground with a man whose main interest was to get away from civilization and from her?

She braced her arms against the hard ground and looked around. She was entangled with a man who was unavailable. He'd made that perfectly clear. He'd chosen a life-style that precluded having a woman share it. And she wasn't going to get burned again. Very carefully, she untangled herself from Adam, then she sat back on the grass a safe distance away and brushed off flecks of dirt from the pants he'd borrowed from Laurie. Out of the corner of her eye, she saw that Adam had propped himself on one elbow, stuck a blade of grass between his teeth and was giving her a look she couldn't fathom.

"We didn't finish what we started," he observed, breathing hard.

"And we're not going to," she told him.

"Not even lunch?" He jumped to his feet with the agility of a panther and pulled her up by the hand, and she realized that he was going to pretend nothing had happened. Or that what had happened was just some lighthearted fun. While she was in danger of losing her heart, he was just having a good time.

She didn't answer. She didn't trust her voice. She just le
him pull her up the hill by the hand. Let him take his plac
under the tree, pick up his sandwich and resume eating as i
nothing had happened. For him, nothing *had* happened
just a romp in the grass. She had to learn not to take thing
so seriously; had to stop trembling like a leaf in the breeze

She had to remember Adam was on vacation and she wa
part of the entertainment. She forced herself to finish he
sandwich, but she didn't taste it. She washed it down wit
mineral water, realizing she had to keep her wits about he
from now on. There would be no more good times at he
expense. She didn't want to be anyone's R and R. The onl
kind of man she was interested in was someone like Jack
someone who was looking for a year-round, full-time, pe
manent relationship—in other words, marriage. Adar
didn't even believe in it. Which reminded her, she hadn'
even finished reading Jack's letter. That was Adam's faul
He'd kept her so busy she hadn't had a minute to herself.

Back at the car, Adam yawned again and Mandy offere
to drive.

"Thanks," he said. "I need a nap."

"Aren't you even going to look at the scenery?" she aske
as he got in next to her and let his head fall back against th
headrest. Why had they come all this way if he was just g
ing to sleep on the way home? But he didn't answer. He ju
closed his eyes and promptly fell asleep while she drov
down the two-lane road that led to the freeway and acro
the Golden Gate Bridge. She wanted to wake him to poi
out Angel Island and Alcatraz, but she didn't.

Occasionally she sneaked a look at his face, noting ho
the taut lines around his mouth softened in sleep, and ho
his forehead was smooth under his dark hair. His hea
bounced from side to side and she wondered how he coul
possibly sleep through that. As the car curved onto Par
side Drive, she felt his body lean toward her and his hea

land on her shoulder. She tried to push him over toward the window, but found she couldn't manage it. Or maybe she wasn't trying very hard, because the masculine scent of his hair and skin filled her senses and left her unable to do anything but drive and think about what had taken place back there in the grass. It would be better if he were awake and talking. It would be much better if his head weren't nestled against her shoulder. But he slept on while she daydreamed until she pulled up in front of her house.

She turned off the motor and he lifted his head from her shoulder, shaking his shaggy head like a seal on the rocks below her house. "Was that a dream or did I really sleep on your shoulder all the way home?" he inquired with his eyes at half-mast, his face inches from hers. Mandy reached behind her, opened the car door and slid out without answering.

He knew perfectly well where he'd slept all the way home. And he knew she could have pushed him away if she'd really wanted to. She took the grocery bag from the back seat and walked to the front door without a backward glance.

Her goal was to get their relationship back on the proper footing—back to a guest-host relationship. An unusual guest, certainly, one who served her breakfast in bed, but still a guest. A guest whom she found extremely attractive. She wasn't afraid to admit she desired him. But only in a physical sense. In every other way he was inferior to, say, someone like Jack, whose personality shone through his letters, whose character was impeccably honest. Someone who wanted the same things she did—love and marriage. Wait a minute. Did Jack want her? He'd never said that. But she hadn't read his last letter. Not yet.

She set the groceries on the kitchen table and turned to find that Adam had followed her into the kitchen. She backed up against the refrigerator and gripped the handle. How was it that he filled the room so completely? This large, spacious kitchen, filled it with his broad shoulders, his rumpled shirt and wrinkled khakis?

While she watched, he unpacked the paper bags and laid the ingredients on the table. "What can I do to help?" she asked with a glance at the onions, tomatoes, mushrooms and meat sprawled out in front of them.

"Nothing." He lifted the cleaver with one hand and tore open the package of beef. "I'll get things started and then I'll pick up the group at the airport."

"But... they're my guests."

"But I promised to pick them up. And you just drove all the way home. Don't you have things to do?"

"Yes, sure." Fascinated, she watched as he turned a chunk of beef into small squares, sliced mushrooms into quarters and chopped onions. "What is it?" she asked finally.

"Beef Stroganoff."

She nodded and edged her way around the room toward the door, feeling displaced, discombobulated and more than a little disturbed. He was in control, just as he had been since the moment he'd arrived, and there was nothing she could do about it. "I'll be in my room," she said. "If you need anything, call me."

Adam nodded absently, and tossed the meat into a smoking pan. He was glad to have something to do besides think about Mandy, because thinking about Mandy led to kissing Mandy and that was wrong. It was the kind of activity Jack would definitely not approve of. The kind of thing Adam wouldn't approve of if *he* were in the Yukon and Jack were here. He shouldn't have done it. He shouldn't have come, and if he had the sense God gave a mongoose, he'd leave right now.

He knew enough right now to settle the question of Mandy. He knew she was sweet and kind and caring, open and funny... He could still hear her laughter echo in his head as they had rolled down the hill together. If he walked out right now and didn't come back, he'd never forget the sound of it, like musical bells, it had been.

He stirred the meat and added some herbs. As he worked, his plan clarified in his mind. He would leave tomorrow morning after the guests took off. That would be the logical time to go. So all he had to do was to get through the evening, and tomorrow he could leave with a sense of accomplishment. He'd been able to help her out and, best of all, he'd thrown her together with Jack. Now the only thing standing in their way was the small matter of Jack's not being a millionaire. And Julie from Illinois. But Julie couldn't compare to Mandy and Mandy didn't need a million dollars to be happy. She only needed someone to love her, to make her feel special, to heal her wounds. Jack could do that. Of course, he could.

He turned down the stove, left the mixture to simmer and went upstairs to change his clothes. Before he left, he tacked a note on Mandy's door with last-minute instructions. The music coming from behind her door was the B52's "Love Shack." He pictured her reading Jack's letter while she listened to the music, while she pictured herself and Jack somewhere in the Yukon in a love shack. He clenched his jaw.

If he knocked on her door, would she open it, would her blue eyes be dreamy, her mind on Jack? He didn't want to find out. He took off for the airport before he did something stupid.

Mandy sat cross-legged in the middle of her bed. She didn't hear Adam chopping away in the kitchen. She didn't hear him come to her door. Not with the music throbbing. She was reading and rereading Jack's latest letter. It wasn't the same as the other letters. It was more eager, more certain about how he felt about her. He wanted to exchange pictures. Mandy didn't know what to do. She told herself it wasn't important what he looked like.

At least, it *hadn't* been important until Adam had arrived and set the standard for what the Yukon man should look like. Maybe she'd be disappointed when she found out Jack didn't look like Adam. A thought that made her feel guilty and shallow for placing so much importance on looks.

She changed her clothes, read Adam's instructions and then went to the kitchen to toss the salad and heat the rolls. She set up the table in the living room and lit a fire in the fireplace. She was setting out the sherry when the guests pulled up. Opening the front door, she greeted the two couples warmly.

Adam brushed by her with their suitcases and muttered into her ear as he passed, "The daughter and her husband are vegetarians."

"Oh, no."

He shrugged and carried their bags upstairs. Mandy made polite conversation. Meanwhile her brain took an inventory of the kitchen and came up with nothing suitable for vegetarians.

"Is it true your husband does the cooking?" the older woman asked Mandy.

"No," she said quickly. "I mean, yes, but . . ."

"Mandy," Adam said from the staircase, "could I have a word with you in the kitchen?"

"Of course. If you'll excuse me for a second, just help yourself to some more sherry."

Once inside the kitchen door, Mandy ran her hands through her hair. "What are we going to do?" she demanded in a stage whisper. "Are you sure they're vegetarians?"

"Positive, but don't worry about it."

"Don't worry about it? Why didn't they tell you this on the phone?" She could feel the panic rise in her throat.

There was a knock on the kitchen door and the younger woman stuck her head in the door. "What time is dinner?" she asked.

Mandy gave Adam a frantic look. "In an hour," he said smoothly.

"Good, then we'll have time for a nap." And the woman closed the door firmly behind her.

Mandy collapsed onto the kitchen chair. "What is it about this place that sends people to bed the minute they arrive?"

Adam leaned against the cabinet and grinned at her. "It's the atmosphere. Everyone feels it. You've created a love shack."

She felt a flush creep up her cheeks as she rubbed at a stain on the table. "I shouldn't complain. As long as they pay their bill, what do I care what they do while they're here? But what on earth are we going to feed them, after you've made your delicious beef Stroganoff?" She sniffed the air and then sighed deeply.

"Omelets?" he asked.

She shook her head.

"Salad?"

"That's all?"

"And pasta," he suggested.

Mandy handed him an apron and put one on herself. "Fine."

They worked steadily for the next hour, shredding lettuce, toasting croutons, grating cheese, boiling noodles, bumping elbows, stepping on each other's toes. Adam muttered instructions, Mandy followed them. When they'd finished, they'd used every pot, every bowl, every utensil in the kitchen. Despite their aprons, they were liberally spotted with globs of cream and butter from head to toe, and the floor looked like the aftermath of a tornado.

Mandy was just spinning lettuce leaves dry when she heard a loud knocking on the front door and a loud voice call, "Anyone home?"

Adam looked at Mandy. Mandy let the lettuce spinner slide across the tiled counter. "Another guest?" Adam asked.

Mandy shook her head. "Laurie."

As if on cue, Laurie burst through the kitchen door in her maroon uniform like a whirling dervish. Setting her small black suitcase down, she opened her arms out wide and yodeled, "I'm ho-ome."

"Great," Mandy said. "Just in time."

"What's for din—" she began, and then she noticed Adam. "Is this the . . . ?"

"This is Adam Gray. Adam, my sister, Laurie."

Laurie extended her hand. "Adam, it's a pleasure. I've heard so little about you. Are you the one . . . ?"

"From the Yukon," Mandy said.

"How exciting."

As they shook hands Mandy noticed Laurie giving Adam a very close examination. "Laurie, we're just about to serve dinner," Mandy said.

"If I'd known, I wouldn't have eaten on the plane. It smells heavenly." She frowned. "But you don't do dinners. And Adam is a guest."

"Yes, I know, but this was a special request. And I can't afford to turn anyone down."

Laurie nodded. "I'm going to change. Back in a minute."

Mandy watched her pick up her bag and leave the kitchen, marveling as she always did at how Laurie could look so perfectly groomed, so well put together, after hours of traipsing up and down the aisle of a 747 and smiling, smiling, smiling.

When Mandy finished the salad, she carried it into the living room, noticing how much the place suddenly resembled a cozy restaurant, with the fire burning in the fireplace and the candles on the table.

She almost ran into Adam on her way back to the kitchen as he came through the door with a bottle of Burgundy. She paused to watch him hover over the table much as he'd done the night he'd arrived, when he'd played maître d' and she was the guest. He was an amazing man, switching identities with the greatest of ease, keeping her amused, entertained, and just a little off balance. And she felt a pang, just for a moment, as she stood there admiring his suave manner, a longing for the dinner in her kitchen with just the two of them, no guests, no sister.

What was wrong with her? She was full to overflowing with guests and she was longing for the good old days when she was half-empty. The truth was that Adam filled up the place all by himself. With him there she forgot all about guests. And right now she'd almost forgotten about the sauce simmering on the stove and the noodles boiling in the pot. She rushed back to the kitchen to take charge.

It seemed to take hours for them to serve and for the guests to eat, but when they'd finished, and the well-fed, contented guests had toddled happily up the stairs to bed, Mandy fell onto the sofa and Laurie walked in the front door in blue jeans and a sweatshirt.

"Where is everybody?" Laurie asked in a loud whisper.

Mandy, almost too tired to speak, pointed one hand toward the second floor, the other toward the kitchen.

Laurie nodded and sat next to her sister on the couch. "Good heavens, why didn't you tell me he was God's gift from the Yukon?"

Mandy smothered a smile. "You didn't ask me."

Laurie crossed her legs underneath her. "Maybe they all look like that. Even Jack. Maybe it's the air or the cold weather."

Mandy leaned her head back against the couch and closed her eyes. "What Jack looks like is not important. What *is* important is that he's honest and faithful." Mandy didn't see Adam come into the living room, but she felt Laurie's sharp dig with her elbow. Her eyes flew open.

"Sounds like man's best friend," he commented, looking at Mandy.

"We were talking about a friend of Mandy's," Laurie explained. "Another Yukon man. I don't suppose you know Jack, do you?"

"We've already been through that," Mandy said. "It's a big territory."

"Sounds like a great guy," Adam said, jabbing the log in the fireplace with a poker.

"He's looking for a wife," Laurie said.

Mandy shifted uncomfortably. "I don't really think Adam's interested in what Jack is looking for."

"Not interested," Adam repeated brusquely. "But don't let that stop you. You two go right ahead and discuss him while I clear this mess out of here."

Mandy jumped to her feet. "No, you sit down while I clean up."

Laurie untangled her feet from the sofa. "Why don't we all work together and get it done faster?"

"Laurie, you go to bed. You must be exhausted from serving meals to two hundred people." Mandy wanted to give her sister a nudge in the direction of the door. There was no telling what she'd say. She might tell Adam that Mandy had met Jack through *Yukon Man*, that Mandy was in love with Jack, or that Mandy was perfect for Adam. But Laurie was determined to stay.

Before they adjourned to tackle the kitchen, Laurie asked Adam where he was going to sleep. He shrugged and pointed to the couch. Mandy ran her hand through her tangled hair. It didn't seem fair for Adam to cook the dinner, wash the dishes and then sleep on the couch. But what could she do? There was a brief pause while she looked at Laurie, who was looking at Adam, who was looking at Mandy, then they all trooped into the kitchen.

Mandy washed, Adam dried and Laurie put away. Laurie told stories about the charter flight she'd worked the night before, about spilled drinks, inebriated passengers, and the three of them were soon laughing and talking as if they'd known each other for years.

When Laurie finally put the last glass away, said goodnight and went to her room, the house was suddenly quiet. The dining table had been returned to its place under the window and Mandy reached into the hall closet for a pillow and a blanket.

"Your sister's a great girl," Adam noted, taking the bedding from her arms.

Mandy nodded. "She thinks you're nice, too." She could hardly say "She thinks you're God's gift from the Yukon," but she thought it. "Thanks again, Adam," she said. But before he wrapped himself in the blanket and settled his long, lanky body into the narrow confines of the couch, she hurried down the hall and closed her bedroom door behind her. After all, there was just so much guilt, longing and gratitude a woman could handle.

Chapter Six

Mandy got up early the next day and noticed right away that the living room was back to normal, with the blanket folded neatly at the end of the couch. Adam was nowhere in sight, but his rental car was parked in front of the house, right next to Laurie's own Toyota. She headed for the kitchen, where she made omelets for the two couples, who then carried their suitcases downstairs. She called a cab to take them back to the airport for their flight to Los Angeles.

Fighting off an urge to go out and look for Adam, who couldn't have gone far without his car, Mandy loaded the dishwasher and poured herself a cup of coffee. She took it out onto the patio where she could watch the sea gulls swoop over the water and ponder her future and the future of the Miramar Inn. If she were full every night, she'd be a financial success. But if she were full every night, how could she manage all by herself?

She could barely manage with the help of Adam and Laurie. And if she were full every night, would she have time for pumpkin festivals or visits to wineries? Not that it mattered, when Adam left she'd have no reason to go off sightseeing, no reason to have fun. Nobody to have fun with. She'd never minded before. Never knew what she was missing. She had tilted her metal chair back against the wall of the house when Laurie came shuffling sleepily through the kitchen door in sandals and shorts.

"Have you seen my white linen pants?" she asked, setting her coffee and a croissant on the table.

"I borrowed them," Mandy confessed. "But they're... they've got a few grass stains on them. I'm going to have them cleaned for you."

Laurie wrinkled her nose. "Grass stains?" She looked around the brick patio. "From where?"

Mandy bit her lip. "From some grass, of course. Why, do you need them right away?"

"No, I just wondered. I'm still wondering. How did you get grass stains on my pants?"

Mandy was spared an answer to the question by the arrival of Adam at the garden gate. He was breathless from a run on the beach and the long climb up the rickety stairs. The sun was in his eyes, his hair was windblown, the muscles in his legs rippled and his feet were bare. He looked like Triton, the Greek god, rising from the sea.

"Beautiful day," he remarked, looking straight at Mandy.

She stood, wiped her palms against her old denim shorts and tried to control her racing pulse. How could one man radiate so much energy and pure animal magnetism so early in the morning? "What can I get you for breakfast?"

He put his hands on her shoulders and gently pushed her back into her seat. "I'll get it." Then he went into the kitchen and Laurie did an exaggerated double-take.

"This man is more at home here than I am. How long did you say he's been here?"

"A few days," Mandy said, holding her coffee cup in front of her face.

"I know how you feel about Jack, Mandy, but don't you think you ought to give Adam a second look?"

"A second look? I haven't given him a first look," she lied. "Laurie, he's just a guest. I can't go throwing myself at the guests, can I? I mean, hostesses have to have some scruples."

"Why, what did you do, take an oath?" Laurie demanded.

"No, but it's understood. Besides, he's not interested in a relationship and neither am I. He was married once and he's been burned. He's going off to work on some oil-drilling platform in the North Sea or the North Slope or something. No women, no nothing. That's his choice. So even if I *were* interested in him, which I'm not, there's no future in it."

"He's interested in you, though." Laurie took a bite of croissant and chewed thoughtfully.

Mandy set her cup down. "I suppose your experience in air travel gives you extra insight into these complicated social relationships?" Mandy asked dryly. "How do you know?"

"It doesn't take a psychoanalyst to tell that Adam has the hots for you," Laurie said matter-of-factly. "Even a lowly flight attendant can detect electricity when it's crackling through the air."

"I told you, it doesn't matter. Even if it's true, he's not going to do anything about it."

"What about you, why don't you do something about it?" Laurie asked. "Don't tell me, I know. You're afraid of getting hurt again. Mandy, that was three years ago. You can't bury yourself in this house as if it were your security blanket. Someday you're going to have to come out and take a look around. And you may find something you like. *Someone* you like. Someone who's honest, who's got integrity and who likes you back. Look what happened when you took a chance and wrote a letter to someone you didn't know. But Jack is just a pen pal, thousands of miles away. Adam is right here under your own roof. And he's a living, breathing hunk. I can't believe you haven't noticed."

"You think he's good-looking?" Mandy asked.

Laurie rolled her eyes. "Of course I think he's good-looking. But he's not looking at me. I might have been a nasturtium on the fence for all he noticed. Yes—" Laurie raised her eyebrows and looked pointedly in the direction of the kitchen door "—the nasturtiums are doing very well."

Mandy turned to see Adam carrying a stack of toast on a plate, along with jam and butter. He set it all in the middle of the table, pulled a wrought-iron chair up and sat down.

"Wait a minute," Laurie said, giving Adam a scrutinizing look. "You've got something on the back of your pants. It looks like grass stains."

Adam shrugged. "Probably. I'll change after breakfast."

"There's not much grass around here," Laurie commented.

Mandy met Adam's gaze over a piece of toast and saw a gleam in his eye and watched a slow smile spread across his face. She felt the corners of her mouth turn up in response. Yes, she knew how the grass stains got there and so did he. And no, she wouldn't forget the smell of the grass, the sound of the wind in the trees and the taste of his lips on hers. But it should be illegal for a man to look at a woman like that, especially at breakfast, especially at her.

She didn't have the defenses required to fight off the way he made her feel, as if a meltdown was taking place in the core of her body. She thought of getting up and going into the kitchen, but she couldn't. Her legs were made of lead, and her arms of graphite. It was all she could do to hold up a piece of toast. She couldn't possibly swallow it. Was it . . . could it possibly be true that Adam was interested in her?

Yes, but only as a short-term amusement. That was what Laurie didn't understand. Or if she understood, she didn't care. But Mandy did. She was not prepared to be dumped again. Once was enough in this lifetime.

Laurie sat drinking her coffee, her gaze traveling between Mandy and Adam, a smug I-told-you-so expression on her face.

Adam drained his coffee cup and set it on the table. "I'll be checking out today," he said abruptly, the smile gone from his face, the gleam in his eyes dimmed.

Mandy blinked as she was hit with an intense feeling of disappointment.

Laurie's eyes widened. "So soon? Is it the couch? Because I'll be gone tonight. You can have your choice of rooms."

"No, it's not the couch. The couch was fine. It's my boss. I've got an appointment to see him. My vacation's over, I'm afraid. I'm going to get a new assignment." There was a brief silence while Laurie waited. "On a drilling platform in the North Sea," he continued.

"That sounds dangerous," Laurie said.

Mandy felt as if she were watching a scene from a movie, one that she'd seen before, one that didn't have a happy ending.

"A little dangerous," Adam admitted, "but we don't go out when the winds kick up above one fifty."

"Oh. That's good." Laurie stood and grabbed an empty plate. "It was good to meet you, Adam. I wish you could stay longer, but maybe you'll be back one of these days. A man always needs some R and R, don't you think? An opportunity to add a few grass stains to the seat of the pants.'' She smiled sweetly, but didn't wait for an answer. She just walked into the house and let the back door close behind her.

Adam wasn't watching Laurie. His eyes were on Mandy. He wished she'd say something. Was she sorry to see him go, or relieved? He couldn't tell. Maybe she was counting the minutes until she could get back to her correspondence with Jack. The disturbing news he'd heard when he'd called Jack this morning was that Julie from Illinois was on her way to the Yukon with all due haste. And with only one thing in mind. To trap Jack and his million dollars. Unfortunately, Jack didn't see it that way. He was sure she loved him for himself, or she would, as soon as she got to know him better.

Adam's goal was to prevent that. He intended to get his own future on track and then head up there to the Yukon so Jack could escape the clutches of Miss Illinois and get down here to see Mandy. Because once he saw Mandy, nobody else would have a chance.

''I'd like to come back someday,'' Adam said, drawing his eyebrows together thoughtfully, ''but I don't know when.''

''You'll be a long way away,'' Mandy agreed readily. So readily, Adam felt a pain in the vicinity of his heart. Wouldn't she miss him at all?

''It's not that,'' he protested. ''It's just that I know it won't be the same. And I want to remember the place...and you...the way you are.'' He stared at her, trying to memorize the way her hair curled lazily around her face, the gently curved line of her cheek, her blue eyes that reflected the cloudless sky above. He knew he wasn't ever going to see her again, not if things went the way they should.

If Jack wanted him in on the wedding, he would say he was busy. The thought of her in a white dress standing under the trellis in the garden with Jack at her side made him feel sick. But he had to do what he could to make it happen. Because it was the right thing. The *best* thing for the both of them. Mandy would make a great wife . . . for Jack. And Jack would adore Mandy just the way Adam did, maybe more. No, not more.

Adam reached across the table and ran his finger along the curve of Mandy's cheek, tracing the soft outline to imprint it on his mind forever. Then he deliberately drew his hand back. He got to his feet and scraped his chair across the bricks. "Thanks for everything," he said in a voice he scarcely recognized as his own. He'd intended to shake her hand or wave or make some noncommittal gesture, but impulsively he pulled her up out of her chair by the elbows and slanted a kiss across her lips. Her lips were cool at first, like the breeze off the ocean, then they warmed and softened and he felt he was in terrible danger of being swept away by her sweetness.

But he was never one to walk away from danger. And no other danger felt so good in his arms, smelled like flowers or tasted like homemade jam. "Mandy," he muttered, pulling back. "I don't want to leave."

She didn't answer for a long moment. Then she linked her arms around his neck and looked up at him with those wide blue eyes. "Then don't," she said softly.

She made it sound so simple. If she only knew why he was there, she'd have kicked him out long ago. If he left now, she might never know. And he *would* leave. After one more kiss. One goodbye kiss. Surely he owed himself that much. He pulled her close to him, so close he could feel her heart pounding through her T-shirt. The kiss went on and on. He put his soul into it, knowing it would be the last, and so did she. Her breasts were pressed against his chest, her bare thighs against his.

The kiss went on and on until he couldn't tell who was kissing whom, or who was giving and who was getting. Was it because they both knew it was goodbye? Was it because they had nothing to fear, nothing to lose? His hands drifted under the hem of her shirt, wanting more. He slid his fingers up against her bare breasts, cupping them. Small murmurs of pleasure came from the back of her throat.

The patio spun around them and her words echoed in his ears. *Then don't... Then don't...* But the cries of the sea gulls overhead warned him, just in the nick of time, to pull away. Reluctantly he broke the kiss and her face swam into focus. He didn't speak. He couldn't. He tried to smile, but it felt as if his face would crack under the strain. Instead he put one foot in front of the other and walked into the house and out the front door.

It wasn't so bad once he started driving, once he started thinking about moving on, moving north, putting some distance between Mandy and himself. The pain in his chest was really quite bearable, especially when he told himself he was doing it for Mandy. She needed someone like Jack, to love her, to take care of her, and most of all, to marry her. She couldn't take another disappointment, and that was all she could expect from Adam.

Yes, he'd gotten out of there just in time. He could still taste her lips and feel the soft weight of her breasts in his hands, the velvet of her cheek against his. He didn't want to care about her. He didn't want her to care about him. That wasn't why he'd gone there. He hoped she wasn't thinking about him as much as he was about her. He wondered what she was thinking about, what she was doing and who was staying there tonight. It wouldn't be long before Jack was there, staying in Adam's room, having breakfast in bed... Adam gripped the steering wheel so tightly his knuckles were white. He'd gotten out of there in time, but just barely.

* * *

The office of Parvo Petrochemicals was located in an office park in the industrial area of the San Francisco Bay. There was an expanse of green lawn out in front, and a fountain that spouted recycled water. Inside there was a secretary who worked for several small companies in the complex. Adam announced himself and then went into the small office of his boss, Gene Perking.

Gene held out his hand, but didn't get up from behind his desk. When Adam shook his hand, Gene winced. "Good to see you. Sorry, I can't get up."

Adam took the chair that faced the desk. "What's wrong?"

"Hernia."

"What? Why don't you do something about it?"

"I am. Just waiting for you to show up. Couldn't trust anyone else to fill in for me."

"Fill in... Oh, no. I'm on my way up to the Yukon, to fill in for Jack. He's counting on me. Isn't there someone else?"

"Nobody else. And don't worry about old Jack. I took care of that."

"You sent someone up there?"

"Yep. Jack was getting antsy."

"I know. When did you talk to him?"

"Just hung up. He's got some woman up there with him."

"Already?" Adam's heart sank.

"Says he wants to marry her."

"No, he doesn't," Adam jumped to his feet. "I've got to stop him."

Gene leaned forward and clutched his side. "Take me to the hospital first. As soon as I bring you up to speed on our operations."

Adam listened with half an ear to Gene's explanations. Meanwhile his mind was on Jack. What was wrong with him? He'd told Jack that Mandy was the one. As soon as he got Gene into the hospital, he'd get Jack on the phone and talk some sense into him.

But it took the rest of the day to check Gene into the hospital, call Gene's ex-wife, and get his last-minute instructions for running the business. Before Adam left him, Gene was wrapped in a hospital gown and a nurse was drawing blood out of his arm with a needle. His boss raised his free hand, told Adam he appreciated what he'd done, and handed him the keys to his house.

"Make yourself at home," Gene instructed. "And I won't forget this. Whatever you want, just ask."

"You know what I want. A job on a drilling platform."

Gene nodded and waved him away. "We'll talk later. Take good care of Elvis."

Adam hesitated. It wasn't a good time to talk about his future with the company, not when Gene was going under the knife the next day. So he promised he'd look after Elvis, and went back to the office. Since most of their operations were in faraway parts of the world, it was a good time to make calls and send faxes. And he certainly didn't want to go back to Gene's house and stare out the windows at the view of the bay with only Elvis for company.

He spun around in Gene's chair and surveyed the map of the world that covered the wall. It was dotted with red flags, each denoting one of Parvo's installations. He stared at the one of the Yukon River for a long time before he called Jack. Then he waited an eternity for Jack to answer.

"What's this I hear about you and Julie?" Adam demanded.

"News travels fast," Jack said in a lazy drawl. "She's here and I'm in love. Is that what you heard?"

"I don't believe it. You just met her. You don't know her. And what about Mandy? You haven't met Mandy."

"I don't need to. I've got Julie."

"Does she know you're not a millionaire?"

"Not exactly."

"That's what I thought. Maybe you'd better tell her before you make any wedding plans."

"I can't tell her now, she's in the kitchen. But I can tell you one thing, she's not a gold digger. As soon as my replacement comes, I'm outta here, man."

"When's that going to be?"

"I don't know. We just had a big storm and everything's grounded. Julie got in just in time. Wasn't that lucky?"

"Very," Adam said dryly. "We have to talk."

"Yeah, sure. But not about me and Julie. We're in love."

"You can't be in love with somebody you just met," Adam explained patiently.

"What do you know about it?" Jack demanded.

"Nothing," Adam admitted, then he said goodbye and hung up. What *did* he know about love? All he knew was that he couldn't keep his mind on the operations of Parvo Petrochemicals because his brain was stuck on the other side of the coastal hills. He was wondering what Mandy was doing tonight. Had she gone back to wallpapering in a loose T-shirt and shorts, or was she sitting on the couch in front of the fire sipping sherry while he sat here in Gene's swivel chair calling outposts from Saudi Arabia to Norway?

Were there guests in his bed, in his upstairs room with the view of the ocean? Would she serve them breakfast in bed the way she'd done for him? He ground his teeth together at the thought of her appearing in her white apron first thing in the morning in front of anyone but him. And yet here he was urging Jack to drop Julie and hustle himself to the Miramar Inn for the purpose of considering Mandy. Was he crazy? Was he too nice for his own good?

No. Mandy deserved happiness, love and security, just what Jack was offering. Only he was offering them to the wrong woman. Arranging transcontinental shipments seemed a breeze compared to arranging these people's lives, but he had a responsibility to do what he could.

Mandy was not serving anyone breakfast in bed, not the next day or the day after that. Last week's boom had turned into this week's bust. Laurie had flown off to St. Louis and no guests had checked in since Adam had checked out last week. No one came, no one called. Mandy had fooled herself into thinking business was on the upturn. Instead, last week had just been an aberration, and now she was back to normal, which was to say she was back to nothing. Yes, she could have gone back to the wallpaper project, but what was the point, if there was no one to appreciate it? She could have replanted her flower boxes, too, but why bother?

She didn't hear from Jack, and of course she didn't hear from Adam. She wouldn't. He was probably bobbing around on an oil platform in the North Sea and out of touch with the whole world. Just the way he wanted it.

Then, to top it all off, just when she thought things couldn't get any worse, she got a "Dear Mandy" letter from Jack. In it he explained he was to marry one of his other correspondents, but that he'd always treasure their friendship.

Mandy gripped the mailbox for support with one hand and crumpled the letter in the other. Friendship? Was that all it had meant to him? While she'd fooled herself into thinking he was serious about her, he'd been serious about someone else. It was happening all over again. She felt so stupid that tears sprang to her eyes. She could have sworn she was more than just a friend to Jack.

But she was wrong. Again. Last week there were two men in her life. And now there was no one. There never *had* been anyone, she reminded herself as she walked up the front steps, her eyes downcast. When she heard the phone ring, she threw the letter into the wastebasket and ran to her desk.

"Miramar Inn," she said in a quavery voice.

"Mandy, this is Adam Gray."

"Are you calling me from your drilling platform?" she gasped.

"No, not yet. I'm over here at the office for a while, doing some desk work for my boss."

"At the office, in Menlo Park?" Suddenly she was forced to revise her image of Adam as a windblown figure on an oil rig to Adam in a suit and tie in an office.

"Yes. My boss went in for surgery last week so I'm stuck here for a while." There was a long pause. "How are you?"

"Fine," she lied.

"Anything happening?" he asked.

"Not much." Why on earth was he calling? she wondered. What was he getting at?

"How's your friend in the Yukon?"

"He's fine. He's getting married. That's good news." She was proud of the way she kept her voice steady.

"What? Where'd you hear that?"

"From him, of course."

"It won't last," Adam predicted.

"How can you be so cynical? For your information, Jack is quitting his job and moving to the States. He's going to give his marriage a chance." She couldn't help this dig at Adam, who didn't seem to realize that marriage required compromises. Not that Mandy knew anything about marriage. At least Adam had made it to the altar. Mandy had never even gotten that far.

"Was that his future wife's idea, quitting his job?"

"I couldn't say," she said coolly. She would never let on to anyone how much she'd cared about Jack, how sad she was to let him out of her life. "I think I hear someone at the door," she said quickly. "I'd better go."

"Keep in touch," he said, and he gave her his office number before he hung up.

She sat at her desk staring at the telephone for a long time, wondering why on earth he'd called, anyway, and why he'd asked about Jack. She hoped he didn't think she was still dreaming about his goodbye kiss, still reliving every intoxicating moment. She would never understand how he could kiss her like that and then forget all about it, act so casual on the phone, as if it—they—had meant nothing to him.

The answer came to her in a flash. Because it *had* meant nothing to him. He probably had forgotten all about it. While she replayed the scene over and over in her mind like a broken record, he'd just moved on with his life. Which was exactly what she should do. The problem was that everything reminded her of Adam. The wallpaper in the bathroom, the sheets on the bed where he'd slept, the stove he'd cooked dinner on, the patio and the beach and on and on. For once in her life she wished she were a flight attendant like Laurie and could fly off to some exotic spot like Toledo. Anyplace but here.

On Sunday it was too cool to have breakfast on the patio, so she sat at the kitchen table. She opened the Sunday newspaper to the travel section, to dream about going to Hawaii and to check out the competition in bed and breakfasts. She skipped to the "Follow the Reader" section, where readers recommended their favorite vacation spots, hotels or tours. And there it was, a letter from a reader about the Miramar Inn.

The letter was signed "Adam Gray." She set her coffee cup down with a bang and smoothed the paper with her thumb and forefinger. First he praised the comfortable rooms, then the view, next the breakfast, and then came the best part.

Owner Mandy Clayton is knowledgeable about local attractions. A charming, gracious hostess, she makes

her guests feel at home. I hated to leave and highly recommend it as a romantic getaway.

Mandy's face flamed with embarrassment. What did he
mean by "romantic getaway"? Did he think she came on to
every single guest? She paced the kitchen floor, then sat
down and read the letter again. Whatever he meant, he
meant it kindly and it was good of him to take the time to
write. She only hoped someone would read it and call to
make a reservation. Which they did. It started Monday
morning. Just one letter to the newspaper and suddenly she
was booked on weekends for the next month. Then she
started filling up the weeknights, too.

When Laurie called her from St. Louis, Mandy shared the
good news. "Adam wrote a letter to the newspaper and all
of a sudden I've got reservations coming out of my ears."

"So he was good for something, that man. Have you
called to thank him, or don't they have phones on drilling
platforms?"

"He's, uh, he hasn't left for his platform yet. He called
me from his office."

"Why?"

"Why? I don't know."

"I do. He's crazy about you."

"Then why did he leave?" Mandy asked.

"Because he had work to do?" Laurie suggested.

"Then why hasn't he come back? It's not that far away."

"I don't know," her sister admitted. "Maybe he's
scared."

Mandy shook her head. "He's going to work in gale-force
winds where men are swept out to sea if they so much as
miss a step. He's not afraid of anything."

"So he's not afraid of physical danger, but maybe he's
afraid of getting hurt in other ways, like you."

"I am not afraid of getting hurt. I just prefer not to. It's called self-preservation."

"Call him back."

"And say what?"

"Say you saw the letter in the newspaper and you want to thank him."

"I could do that," Mandy said thoughtfully, as if she hadn't thought of it herself. As if she hadn't been thinking of it constantly.

"Of course you could. And then he'll say, 'Why don't we get together and take up where we left off? Now that Jack's out of the picture and I'm divorced there's nothing to stand in our way.'"

"And then I'll say, 'But what about your job in the North Sea where no women are allowed?'" Mandy said.

"And *he'll* say that he'll smuggle you into his cabin, bring you leftovers from the dinner table and make mad, passionate love to you in his bunk all night long."

Mandy laughed. "And what about my business? My reservations that won't quit? My chance to finally climb out of the red and into the black? Are you suggesting that I give it all up for a life as a stowaway in the North Sea?"

"You could do worse," Laurie suggested.

"I could do better, too, by staying right here and running a successful operation," Mandy noted.

"You still have to call and thank him."

"I will, but don't get your hopes up, because all he's going to say is, 'You're welcome.' I tell you he's not interested in a relationship. He told me, and I'm telling you," Mandy said emphatically, and hung up. Sometimes she wondered if she repeated these things for Laurie's benefit or her own. Whatever the reason, she reached for the phone before she lost her nerve and dialed the number Adam had given her.

"Parvo Petrochemicals."

"Adam, this is Mandy Clayton," she said all in one breath. "Thank you for sending that letter to the newspaper."

"You're welcome," he said just as Mandy had predicted he would, but she felt a rush of disappointment anyway. "Did it do any good?" he asked.

"Oh, yes. In fact I've got a waiting list for some weekends in December. It's... it's wonderful."

"Your place is wonderful, you deserve to be successful."

"Thank you." Mandy wondered how long she could go on like this, thanking him every other minute.

"What are you doing?" Adam asked, leaning back in his chair and propping his feet on his desk. The sound of her voice brought back memories, memories he hadn't been able to bury sitting at his desk only an hour away. Memories of Mandy on a ladder in a steamy bathroom, Mandy by candlelight. He'd thought that he would forget about her once he got away, but apparently he hadn't gotten far enough. Things would be different when he got out of the office. But Gene was still recuperating, and Adam couldn't upset him by asking him when he could leave.

"Oh, just the usual," Mandy answered. "Painting, papering and planting."

He noticed her voice was smooth and calm. He assumed she'd recovered from Jack's defection over to Julie and that her life was back to normal. If only he could say the same. He was glad he'd sent the letter. She'd thanked him and now he could hang up. But he didn't want to.

"I was just writing a speech," he said, although she hadn't asked him what he was doing. "To give at the U.S. Geological Service monthly meeting."

"How interesting. Can anyone come?"

"Yes, but they don't. Why, would you like to hear it?" he asked hopefully.

"I guess I wouldn't understand it."

"Oh, yes, you would. I'm showing slides, though. Guaranteed to put everyone to sleep."

She chuckled. A warm, funny, intimate sound that made him smile into the receiver. "Doctors recommend my lectures for insomnia. I don't blame you for not wanting to come."

"It's not that..."

"I tell you what. If you're still awake at the end of the lecture, I'll buy you a cup of coffee."

"I might be busy."

"It's on Tuesday, at the headquarters on Middlefield Road. Eight o'clock."

"Can I let you know?"

"You don't have to. There'll be plenty of empty seats."

She thanked him again and hung up, breathless from having heard his voice again after so long. The question was—should she go to Menlo Park, or not?

She hadn't said she would come to the lecture, Adam noted, but she hadn't said that she wouldn't. Though why he wanted her there so desperately, he didn't want to consider. He wanted to see her again more than he cared to admit. The lecture was a good place to see her, even if she did yawn her way through his slides of the Yukon. Then he would say goodbye once and for all. Before long, he'd be on his way. He tilted his head back and looked at the expanse of blue labeled North Sea on the wall map. It looked cold and empty and far away.

Chapter Seven

Adam had given many speeches to many groups and he'd never been bothered by nerves. In fact, he usually enjoyed explaining his job and describing the vast riches that lay under the land and sea. But every time he'd opened his mouth so far tonight, his throat went dry and his stomach felt as if it were bungee jumping from the Golden Gate Bridge. He'd arrived an hour early at the auditorium in the first rainstorm of the season to set up the projector and load his slides.

He stood drumming his fingers on the podium, listening to the rain and the wind, wondering if Mandy would come in this storm and, if she came, where she'd sit. He told himself not to think about her. She wasn't coming because she wasn't interested in the Yukon or in him.

Women found the Yukon cold and remote and unlivable. He'd never forget the look on his ex-wife's face when they'd landed in Whitehorse—shock, disbelief and disgust. And that had been for Whitehorse, the one thriving metropolis of the Yukon.

He wished now he'd never mentioned the lecture to Mandy. He didn't want to see those same emotions on her face when she saw his slides of the frozen northland. He'd rather leave here not knowing that she was like every other woman, including Julie from Illinois, who had forced Jack to quit his job and head for the States. He told himself not to worry. She wasn't going to come. The rain pelted the windows. *Nobody* was going to come. He shuffled his notes and straightened his tie and adjusted the microphone.

By eight o'clock, however, there was a decent crowd filling the seats. Adam inhaled deeply and stopped looking at the double doors at the rear of the auditorium with relentless fascination. He cleared his throat and began his lecture. And then she came. At least, he thought it was her. It was a woman with brown hair in a belted trench coat and knee-high leather boots who stood at the back, in the semidarkness.

He wanted to drop his notes, race back there and throw his arms around her, but he didn't. He kept talking as if nothing had happened. Nothing had, after all. Then why did he stumble over his words and skip two lines of important information? Could it really be Mandy under that coat, or was he hallucinating?

He talked about the history of exploration in the territory, noting, out of the corner of his eye, as she took a seat at the end of the back row. And suddenly he relaxed. Suddenly everything was right, including his jitters and his speech. He told stories of old-timers and grizzled prospectors, and then he showed his slides.

Just watching them gave him a pang of longing to feel the Arctic wind in his face, to breathe the cold air, to see the fir trees bend in the wind and to face the unknown. It was worth the hardships, the discomfort and the loneliness. It was where he belonged and the sooner he left, the better. He turned the lights on and, to his surprise, no one was asleep. Not even Mandy, who was leaning forward in her seat, her eyes glued to his face. He knew what she was thinking. How could anyone want to live there?

The audience clapped and he thanked them. Mandy stood and turned toward the exit. He jumped down from the stage, and wedged his way through the crowd. He finally caught up with her in the lobby and sauntered up to her as if he hadn't panicked, as if she weren't trying to get away before he could talk to her. Just in case she thought about trying, he took her hands and held them in his.

"I'm glad you came," he said as the crowd milled around them.

"So am I. It was a wonderful talk. Thanks for inviting me." She looked at the exit.

He tightened his grip on her fingers. "Wait a minute. What about coffee, or did you fall asleep?"

She shook her head. "Of course not, but I'd better get back. The weather and all."

"I think it's letting up. Come back to the house and I'll make some espresso. It's not that far out of your way."

"Well," she said dubiously, "just for a little while."

He went back to get his equipment, feeling strangely euphoric. The speech was over, Mandy was here, and the heavens were dumping moisture on the earth. Not too much moisture, he hoped, not enough to prevent Mandy from sharing one last cup of coffee.

Outside he found the rain had let up and Mandy agreed to follow him through the wet streets. He drove slowly, keeping her headlights in his rearview mirror as they climbed up into the hills. He turned into Gene's long driveway and parked in front of the two-story house. On a hill, it commanded a spectacular view of the bay. It was dark in the driveway and he reached for her hand when she got out of her car so she wouldn't stumble.

"Nice place," she said, looking up at the tall trees that lined the driveway.

"My boss's," he explained, drinking in her profile as if he'd been dying of thirst. He hadn't forgotten the slight tilt of her nose, her determined chin and full lips, but he'd forgotten the effect she had on him, the feeling that he couldn't get enough of her, no matter how much time he had.

As if she felt the heat from his gaze, she looked at him inquiringly, a smattering of raindrops nestled in her dark hair.

"I've never seen you in a trench coat," he explained. "You look like Mata Hari."

"I've never seen you in a suit," she countered. "You look like James Bond."

He gave her a crooked smile, then led the way up the brick steps as the heavens opened up and threatened to drench them both. He slammed the front door behind them and took her into the high-ceilinged living room. Then he took her wet trench coat from her shoulders and again he was caught staring.

"I've never seen you in a dress before, either." His gaze lingered on the silky fabric that caressed her breasts, that drifted past her hips and ended at midcalf.

She ran her palms down the sides of the dress self-consciously. "I don't usually wear one, so I had to raid Laurie's closet. But I thought... since it was a lecture..."

"You didn't get wet, did you? Do you want to change into something else?" he asked hopefully, picturing her in his terry-cloth robe or a jumbo sweatshirt.

"I'm fine," she said. "But you go ahead."

He looked down at his damp, wing-tip shoes and nodded. Just then a loud, squawking voice came from the rear of the house. "Hello," the voice screamed.

Startled, Mandy jumped.

"That's just Elvis," Adam explained. "Come back an
meet him."

Mandy followed Adam through the living room and dow.
a long hall to a den. When Adam flicked on the lights,
brightly colored tropical bird in a large cage opened hi
enormous bill and chirped, whistled and gurgled at hel
"Love me tender," he demanded.

Adam grinned. "He likes you," he explained. "And s
do I," he added under his breath.

"What is it?" Mandy asked, hovering in the doorway.

"A toucan. My boss brought him back from Sout
America a few years ago and taught him to talk by playin
old Elvis Presley records for him. Don't be afraid. He like
people." Adam bent over and lit a flame to the paper, kir
dling and logs that had been carefully laid in the fireplace
"Elvis is the real reason I'm here and not in the North Sea,'
he said, watching the flames flare. "Gene had surgery las
week, and I'm running the office for him. But when I call i
my daily report, the first thing he asks about is his bird."

Mandy finally left the safety of the doorway and crosse
the room to peer at the bird in the cage. "He's not mal
ried?"

"Elvis? No, and neither is Gene. He was, but his wife go
sick of his traveling. It didn't work out. It never does."

Mandy nodded slowly, noting the bleak look in Adam'
eyes before he turned to stare into the fireplace. Then h
glanced at her. "I'll go change. Make yourself comfort
able."

She watched him leave, then she sank into the large, sol
armchair that flanked the fireplace. "What on earth am
doing here?" she asked, gazing into the bird's beady eyes
But he didn't answer. If he had, he would have told her sh
shouldn't have come. He would have cited the weather an
the unstable condition of her feelings for Adam.

It was bad enough she'd driven over the hills in the rain to see and hear how wonderful the Yukon was, she didn't need to be reminded that marriage to an oil-drilling scientist never worked out. Unless, of course, you married Jack Larue, who was the one man willing to make sacrifices to make his marriage work.

It was a good thing she'd never known what Jack looked like. If he looked anything like Adam she'd have real reason to be depressed. There was no denying that Adam in that suit was sinfully handsome. More Alec Baldwin than James Bond. The man should be sent back to the Yukon before he broke any more hearts. Not that he'd broken hers. It was just... Oh, Lord, she didn't know what was wrong with her. She had all the business she could handle and yet she still wasn't happy. She was sad, lonely, depressed and confused. First there was Jack and then there was Adam.

Both men were from the Yukon, but that was where the resemblance ended. The only other thing they had in common was this strange attraction she felt for both of them. On the other hand, it wasn't so strange. They were the only men in her life, so naturally, being isolated and all, she'd fallen for both of them. But was it natural?

Adam walked back into the room wearing old gray sweats and carrying two small cups of dark, strong coffee in his hands. She stared. So it wasn't the suit that made him so irresistible. It was just him. She hadn't seen him for a week or so and she'd forgotten how broad his shoulders were, how dark and penetrating his eyes were, as if he could see into her heart. Which she sincerely hoped he couldn't.

She certainly didn't want him to know she thought about him all the time, relived that last kiss on her patio, the touch of his hands against her sensitive skin and the slight scratch of his cheek against hers. She took a cup from his hands and managed to keep her hands steady.

"How much longer will you be here, filling in for you boss?"

Adam frowned. "Gene doesn't seem to be recuperating as fast as he should. He's been moved to a rehab center Until he's well, I'm stuck here."

She looked around at the wood-paneled walls, at the well-stocked bookshelves, and sipped her coffee, listening to the drumming of the rain on the roof. "It's not such a bad place to be stuck," she observed, the heat from the fire radiating outward and warming her.

Adam took the chair opposite hers. "No, I can't complain, or I shouldn't complain. But it isn't where I want to be and it's not what I want to be doing." He ran his hand through his damp hair. "I want to get going. Get back to where I belong."

Mandy nodded. "The Yukon is a beautiful place. I understand how you feel about it now."

There was a long silence in the room. The bird was quiet watching them silently from his perch. The fire crackled cheerfully, but outside the wind picked up and howled down the chimney. The pleasant patter of the rain turned into a loud drumming. Mandy shivered. This was crazy. It was worse than crazy. It was torture—sitting here with the world's most attractive, most unavailable man, while he dreamed of getting away from here, and from her, and she dreamed of...what?

She dreamed of being in his arms again, kissing him tangling her hands in his thick, dark hair. But it wasn't going to happen, and she'd driven for an hour for a dose of hard, cold reality. Just what she didn't need. Or maybe she did. What she needed right now was to get out of there, fast She set her coffee cup on the table and stood. Adam looked at her inquiringly. There was a loud crash, the sound of splintering wood and then the lights went out.

Adam jumped to his feet. "Good God, it must have been a tree. Stay here, I'll get a flashlight." He was back in a minute, shone his light at her and took her by·the hand to lead her through the darkened house and out the front door. There, halfway down the driveway, illuminated in the beam of his flashlight, was a giant oak tree, snapped off halfway up its trunk. A tangle of broken power lines lay underneath it.

He aimed his light on the other trees that towered above the house and exhaled slowly. "I guess we're lucky it wasn't one of those. It would have come right through the roof." He looked up as the rain ran down his face.

She pulled her hand from his and pressed her palms together. "How will I get back down the drive?" she asked, ignoring the rain that plastered her dress to her skin.

"Tomorrow I'll call the tree service and the power company. They'll have their hands full tonight."

"Tomorrow?" she asked, blinking back the raindrops that caught in her eyelashes.

"Do you have guests? Do you need to call home?"

"No, not tonight, but..." Her mind was racing. She was so desperate to get away from him she almost jumped over the log in her high-heeled shoes and ran down the road. Where she'd run to, she had no idea. There were no lights on anywhere in the neighborhood.

"The lines could be live," he cautioned, as if he'd read her mind. "It's not safe to go anywhere near them."

She nodded and turned back to the house. But not before Adam noticed the way her shoulders slumped. Was it that awful to contemplate spending the night with him in a big, beautiful house overlooking the bay? Apparently so, by the way she was dragging herself back to the house in the rain.

"There's plenty of room," he assured her. But she didn't answer. She just walked slowly in front of him as the beam of his flashlight picked up the sway of her hips under the wet, clinging fabric of her dress. And suddenly his pulse was racing. Silently they marched through the darkened house single file, Adam now leading the way with the light. They went back to the den. He wanted so badly to reach for her to turn her around and feel the warmth of her body through that cool, wet silk dress.

"Look," he said, switching off the flashlight. "I'm sorry about this, but there's nothing we can do. We're safe, we're dry and we're warm. Or we will be dry once we change clothes."

She looked around the den and gave a little shiver. He ran his hand down her arm. "I'll get you something to wear."

She nodded. Why didn't she say something? he wondered anxiously. Say she wasn't sorry she had to spend the night here with him, say she'd missed him just half as much as he'd missed her. Say she'd at least thought about him during the past week, the way he'd thought about her.

The firelight cast shadows on her face. She looked aloof faraway, as if she'd willed herself to another place. He tossed his flashlight onto the chair. "For God's sake, Mandy, would you say something?" But he didn't give her a chance. Grabbing her, he pulled her close and slammed his mouth against hers in fury and frustration, almost immediately softening the kiss. He'd forgotten how sweet she tasted ... From a distance, he heard her short, sharp intake of breath, felt the shock waves rock her body, and then the two of them were locked together in a wild, wet embrace.

Mandy's knees buckled and she clung to Adam for support. She was not prepared for this. Not prepared to be crushed against him, to feel the welcome heat from his body. When she'd driven over the hills in the rain she had never imagined the evening would end this way. She opened her rain-washed lips and was filled with his warmth and his desire. She wanted more. She wanted all of him. She tightened her arms around him and pressed her breasts against his chest.

He groaned and ran his hands down her back to cup her damp dress, molding her bottom with his palms. Bending down, he quickly removed her boots, then he lifted her up. He shifted her in his arms and she wound her arms around his neck. He took her to the soft, thick rug in front of the fireplace and knelt down next to her. He searched her eyes. He thought he knew, but he had to ask.

"Tell me what you want, Mandy." He was breathing hard and so was she. Her breasts were rising and falling under the soft silk of her dress. He drew a circle around them with his fingers and felt her arch toward him.

She took his face in her hands, her palms against his temples and looked deep into his eyes. "I don't know," she murmured. "I want you, but..."

"I can't help falling in love with you," Elvis admitted from his perch in the corner.

"Shut up," Adam said grimly. "Not you," he assured Mandy, kissing the tender hollow above her collarbone.

"What I want is..." For the life of her she couldn't speak, not with Adam's lips finding every sensitive place he could reach, behind her ear, at the corners of her mouth, at the nape of her neck, until she was filled with a pounding need she couldn't deny. But first she had to explain...something, something she had to tell him. She spread her hands against his chest, sliding her palms up and under the sweatshirt that covered his muscles until she heard him gasp. "I know," she murmured. "There's something I have to tell you..."

"Shut up," he said softly. *"You,"* he said, indicating her this time. And then he kissed her again, a long, slow kiss that made her feel as if she'd been drugged. What did he put in those kisses that made her want so much more?

The next time she came up for air she moved away from him and slid back on the floor, tilting her head against the seat of the overstuffed chair. She took a deep breath. "Adam," she said in a shaky voice. "I haven't been completely honest with you."

His heart stopped. He wasn't in the mood for any true confessions, the reciprocal kind, anyway. He wondered if she was finally going to confess she'd answered an ad in *Yukon Man*. If so, he would have to confess, too, and that was the last thing he wanted to do. He reached out to smooth her damp curls with his hand, sliding the silky strands through his fingers.

"That's all right," he assured her, his voice dropping a notch.

"No, it isn't," she protested. "Because the way I've been acting is...might be... It's about Jack."

Adam groaned. Not Jack. Not again. "Jack has nothing to do with you and me."

She tugged at the hem of her dress, which had crept up to her thighs. "Yes, he does. When I told you I wasn't interested in Jack, it wasn't true. I thought I was in love with him." She took a shaky breath and hurried on. "I know I've never met him, but we wrote to each other for a long time and I really thought—I *knew*—there was something special between us. Do you know what I mean? No, you couldn't possibly know unless it had happened to you. I mean, I told Jack things I've never told anyone else."

Adam nodded understandingly. Who could understand any better than he? He knew about her childhood; how she couldn't refuse a dare; how she'd felt jealous of Laurie...

"It sounds crazy," she continued, "but we were so close, so intimate—without ever even having seen a picture of each other—that I really believed..."

"He'd come and find you someday and you'd live happily ever after," Adam finished, feeling a draft of cold air grip his heart. How could he have done this to her? Make her fall in love with someone who didn't exist?

Mandy smiled sadly. "How did you know? But now I feel so naive, so stupid for believing what I did. It's taken me a while to get over it." She wrapped her arms around her waist, as if she could protect herself from getting hurt again.

Adam clenched his teeth. He hated himself for his part in this mess. Why had he ever agreed to answer her letters? Why had he continued past the point of no return? Curiosity pure and simple. The desire to help Jack was just part of it, but mostly he'd wanted to see what Mandy was like to satisfy his own desire. He had to know if she was anything like her letters. The problem was, she was better. Much better.

She sighed. "What I'm trying to say is that by coming here tonight, coming on to you the way I have..." She paused. "Well, it's only because I'm on the rebound."

"Rebound... from Jack?" he asked incredulously.

"Yes, it's obvious to me now," she said, gazing into the dying embers in the fireplace. "I've been jumpy, irritable and on edge ever since I found out, and I'm not behaving very rationally."

Adam nodded slowly, a sinking feeling in the pit of his stomach growing deeper. "And that's where I come in."

She reached for his hand. "I'm sorry. But it isn't fair to you to go on like this. To lead you on any more than I already have."

"So you think you're taking advantage of me?" he said.

She nodded slowly. "I'm afraid so."

"So you don't think," he said, bracing himself with his arms at his sides on the floor, "that I'd have a chance next to Jack."

"It's like comparing apples and oranges. You're totally different."

That slime. That rotten, no-good, scumbag Jack. How could he have dumped her like that without even seeing her first? Why wasn't he the one who was here with her tonight? On the other hand, if he were, Adam wouldn't have had this last chance to see Mandy. His eyes lingered where the neckline of her dress had slipped to one side and a lacy bra only partially covered her full breasts.

If it weren't for Jack, he'd be lifting her damp dress over her head, unhooking that lacy bra and burying his face in the warmth of her body. The heat rushed to his head and he pulled himself to a standing position, gripping the mantel for support. Once again Jack had stepped between himself and Mandy as surely as if he were there in person. It would have been kinder of Jack to tell her he'd drowned in the Yukon River than to tell her he wanted to marry someone else. The man had no sense of propriety, no understanding of women.

Adam looked down at Mandy's hair gleaming in the firelight. "Now that we've cleared the air," he said, ignoring the fact that while she'd cleared the air, he hadn't, "we can go back to normal."

"Separately," she added. She looked up and met his gaze. "You're going up North and I'm going back home. As soon as I can get down the driveway." She brushed her palms together and got to her feet as if she'd just solved all her problems, and he was forced to let the subject drop.

Adam picked up his flashlight, muttered, "Good night, Elvis," and led the way upstairs to one of the spare bedrooms with a connecting bath. Meanwhile his brain was spinning, trying to follow Mandy's crazy logic. One thing he knew for sure. Mandy didn't deserve to be hurt again, and there was no happy ending at the end of this story. Only happy memories. Is that what he'd have when he got to the North Sea, happy memories of Mandy confessing her love for Jack? Did that really classify as a happy memory? Adam didn't think so.

"I'll leave the flashlight for you," he said, opening the door to the guest room for her. "And I'll get you some clothes. The bathroom's inside. Get yourself a hot bath and warm up." He turned quickly before the image of Mandy in her bath, the soap bubbles cascading over her shoulders, down her breasts and onto her stomach, prevented him from standing upright. He was back in a few minutes.

He knocked and she opened the door, barefoot but still in her wet dress. He gave her a stack of men's clothing, sweats, a thick, terry-cloth robe, socks and moccasins. He said good-night, but she said nothing.

When the door closed behind him, Mandy stood there for a moment in the dark, her outstretched arms piled high with clothes as if she were staying for a week. Then she set them down on the dresser and stumbled into the bathroom, where she'd left the flashlight. She took her dress off and then her lacy bra and panties and slid into the hot tub. It was good to get off the treadmill. Adam did that to her. He did other things, too, like making her feel like a bowl of Jell-O, all cool and sleek and quivery inside.

Now that she'd figured it out, she felt better. She was on the rebound, pure and simple. Nothing else made sense. Certainly not being in love with two men at the same time, one of whom she'd never met, the other she knew nothing about.

Nothing? Not even the way he kissed with his whole soul, the way he felt about women and marriage, the way he cooked, the way he smiled at her, the way he looked in a suit? All superficial, she reminded herself. Whereas her knowledge of Jack was deep and profound, based on months of correspondence, of confiding in each other. But now Jack's depth and understanding were lost to some other woman.

A tear slid down Mandy's cheek. She sank down into the tub until the water was lapping at her chin. It was more than anyone could take, being dumped twice in a lifetime. It was time she got the message. She just wasn't meant to find anyone for a long-term relationship. Take Adam. He was attracted to her, but as soon as he could, he was going to get out of her life.

But this time she was going to get out first. After tomorrow morning, she'd never see him again. No more good-byes. No more last meetings, last meals, last kisses. This was it. Why should she set herself up for another letdown? She wouldn't.

Mandy woke in the morning to the loud buzz of a chain saw. The sun was shining into the room as if there'd never been a storm and she looked around in a daze, wondering for a second where she was and how she'd gotten there. She stretched her arms in the extra-large sleeves of a navy blue sweatshirt. Feeling its soft fleece against her skin, she inhaled the combination of citrus after-shave and leather. *Adam.* She was wearing Adam's clothes and sleeping in Adam's boss's house.

She jumped out of bed and stumbled into the bathroom, where she brushed her teeth and tried to tame her hair. Sitting on the edge of the firm mattress where she'd slept so soundly, she pulled on a pair of thick white cotton socks. The walls of the room were painted pale yellow, she noticed, with a thick, Chinese sculpted rug on the floor. Good taste, this Gene had, or had his long-departed wife decorated the house before she'd left during a bout of loneliness?

Padding softly down the stairs, all Mandy could think of was how quickly she could get out of there. How fast she could escape the relentless charm of Adam Gray. The persistent sound of the chain saw was a good sign. It meant someone was working on the fallen tree. From the front window she saw a crew of hard hats halfway down the driveway and she smiled grimly and went to find Adam.

He didn't hear her coming. He was in the black-and-white tiled kitchen at the rear of the house, feeding the bird. Elvis was standing on a newspaper, next to his cage, stabbing at morsels of food with his big, clumsy bill. As soon as he got something in his mouth he tossed it into the air, then caught it in his beak again. Mandy paused in the doorway and watched him do his trick. Then, to her horror, the toucan began flinging bits of leftover food against the wall. Adam swore loudly and ducked out of the way just in time to miss a glob of mashed banana.

Elvis screeched, "Return to sender," then laughed insanely.

In spite of herself, Mandy joined in the laughter, unable to control herself.

Adam spun around. "Good God, I didn't hear you come in. Couldn't you have said something?"

"I'm sorry," she said contritely. He'd probably forgotten she was even there at all. "I would have just left without bothering you, but . . ."

"You would have left," he said, leaning against the sink and letting his gaze roam over the sweatshirt that came to her knees and the pants that drooped around her ankles, "without saying goodbye to Elvis?" He held out a plum and the bird took it in his giant beak. "He may be lacking in table manners, but, hey, nobody's perfect. Who does he remind you of?"

"Jeremy?"

"That's it. I couldn't remember his name." He grinned. "I'll never forget the look on your face when the little scamp threw his muffin across the floor."

"No one ever did that before," she admitted.

"Wait till you have kids."

"I don't think I'll have to worry about kids," she said. "Not with my luck with men."

"Now wait a minute. All men aren't like Jack."

"Don't you dare say anything about Jack. You don't know him. You don't know why he did what he did." She was protesting too much. She was overreacting, but she couldn't stop.

He froze. Lights flickered from the depths of his dark eyes, then dimmed. He held out his palms and shrugged. "You're right. You're absolutely right. I don't know anything about Jack, but I do know something about you."

She picked up an apple from the fruit basket on the counter and examined it carefully. "You do? What do you know?"

"I know that someday you're going to meet someone you love as much as Jack. Even more. Maybe you've already met him. You just don't know it."

"Did I say I was in love with Jack?" she asked.

"You didn't have to. I was there when you got his letter. I may not be a rocket scientist, but I know love when I see it."

"Really." She polished the apple with the sleeve of her shirt. "So you think I was in love with him?"

He nodded. "I know you. I can see right through you. For example, right now I know you need a big, hearty breakfast. And now that the tree's almost out of the way we can go to my favorite hangout on my way to work."

Mandy looked at him, at his long legs in his well-pressed khakis, his cable-knit-sweater-encased shoulders, and sighed helplessly. What good did it do to protest? He always got his way. And what difference did one last breakfast together make now that she had it figured out? She was rebounding, right? She sighed.

"I'll change back into my dress."

He nodded. "You do that. And I'll clean up the mess."

She left the kitchen and Adam got Elvis back into his cage by bribing him with a bunch of grapes. As he closed the door on the bird, Elvis opened his beak. "Don't be cruel," he lectured.

"I'm not being cruel, you dumb bird," Adam said. "Is it cruel to take her out to breakfast? Is it cruel to help her get over Jack? If anyone's cruel, it's Mandy, holding Jack up to me like a saint. Sure, he's a good guy, but he's not worth the suffering she's going through. All I want to do is boost her morale. Is that cruel?" he asked, washing the wall with a sponge.

Elvis didn't answer. He hopped onto his perch and stared straight ahead, awaiting transport back to the den.

The restaurant was halfway between Gene's house and the office, and Mandy followed Adam in her car. The waitress knew Adam and gave Mandy an inquisitive look as she poured two cups of coffee.

"The usual?" she asked Adam.

"Right, and a special for the lady."

"How did you know?" Mandy asked when the waitress left.

"I know you better than you think," he said with a smile.

She put her elbows on the table. "If you know me so well, then tell me what I'm doing wrong." Her blue eyes were troubled and he wanted to hold her hands in his and tell her she wasn't doing anything wrong. She did everything right, including breakfast, kissing and laughing and talking, walking.

"Are we talking about Jack again?" he asked wearily.

"Only partly. I just wonder what I'm doing that men don't like. What makes them choose someone else every time? Go ahead, you can tell me. I can take it."

He studied her face for a long moment, her cheeks scrubbed clean of any makeup, her fine eyebrows arched over cloudless blue eyes, the proud tilt of her chin, the soft indentation of her throat, and his heart ached.

"Didn't it occur to you that there's nothing wrong with you, it's them?"

"No."

The waitress set two glasses of freshly squeezed juice on the table.

"Neither of the men you're referring to were right for you," he said at last.

"How do you know?" she asked, rubbing her glass with her thumb.

"Because I'm a scientist. Not a rocket scientist, but trained to form hypotheses and make observations. And my observation is that you were too good for those guys. You deserve better."

Her mouth curved into a hopeful smile and her dimple flashed. Suddenly it occurred to Adam, as if a light bulb had gone off over his head, that the only person who was good enough for Mandy was him. It was a brilliantly frightening insight that made his hands shake as he reached for his coffee.

It was just too bad he *wasn't* a rocket scientist with a nine-to-five job testing rockets in the desert. They would have a little house on the air base and he would come home after work to Mandy. But he was a geologist, the kind who was trained to hypothesize and observe and to drill for oil under the earth and sea in the most rugged and demanding conditions. The most exciting kind of work he could imagine, aside from rocket science. The kind that ruled out any kind of personal life, except for an occasional vacation.

Maybe he could come back from time to time, on R and R, of course, and stay at the Miramar Inn with Mandy. He stared into her sky blue eyes and contemplated having a fling with her, then just as quickly dismissed the idea. It had to be a clean break, and it had to be now. Right after she ate her strawberry waffle and right after he finished his toast and eggs. Only suddenly he wasn't very hungry, and could only push the food around on his plate. Fortunately Mandy didn't notice.

A half hour later they stood on the pavement in front of the coffee shop, Mandy in her wrinkled silk dress, her trench coat over her arm. He took a deep breath in preparation for his farewell speech, but Mandy beat him to it.

"Thank you, Adam," she said, reaching for his hand to shake it firmly. "You've been a great help to me, really you have. You've put things in perspective, and you've been good for my ego. Are you sure you're a geologist? You could have been a psychologist. You've got the insight and the right instincts."

He held her hand tightly, not ready to let go. Not yet. He couldn't believe this was the end, the last time he'd ever see her. He fought off a feeling of panic, and searched his mind for something to say. Something meaningful, something memorable. But all he could do was to look at her and try to remember how she looked before she got into her car, her hair tucked behind her ears, the neckline of her dress revealing just a hint of pink lace, reminding him of all the things he wished he'd done but never would.

They stood there for what seemed like hours, her hand in his, but it was probably just a few minutes before she pulled away and crossed the street to her car. Later he thought about the way her eyes glistened, as if she might have even shed a tear or two over him, but that was just wishful thinking. It was actually just as she'd said. He'd been a great help to her, renewed her self-confidence and restored her ego. He could only feel good about that.

But he didn't feel good, he felt awful.

Chapter Eight

When Mandy got home she found a whole bunch of messages on her answering machine. On an ordinary day she would have been thrilled. But thrilled was not what she felt that day. Yes, she felt proud of herself for having figured out what was going on in her head, but it didn't last very long. Pride was quickly replaced by an intense feeling of loneliness.

How she could feel lonely with the house full every night, she didn't know, but she did. One good thing was that she was so busy she didn't have time to stare out the window at the gray-green waters of the Pacific wondering what Adam was doing. The bad thing was that her guests were invariably couples, couples who gazed at each other with adoration. Couples who flirted, teased and touched each other right in front of her.

Mandy tried not to notice, but she couldn't help it. It made her want to be a part of a couple, to touch, to flirt and to tease, the way she had with Adam. There were times she wished he'd never come to the Miramar Inn. There were other times she was just grateful for the happy memories. There were times when she picked up the phone and dialed his office number then hung up. She had no idea what she would have said. Chances were she'd have reached his boss. Chances were Adam was already back in the Yukon, a land so incredibly beautiful, living a life so challenging he wouldn't have time to think of her. It had been two weeks since she'd seem him. Not that she was counting.

While Mandy was washing sheets and baking muffins and trying to be a gracious hostess to couples who scarcely noticed her presence, Adam continued to show up at the office every day, shuffled men and supplies around the world for Gene's company and wished himself anyplace but there.

He didn't hear from Jack. He didn't hear from Mandy. He called her a few times, but he hung up without leaving a message. What message would he have left? "I miss you so much I have a permanent pain in my chest.... I think about you nonstop, especially when I go home to that big, empty house with only a bird for company. A bird that keeps telling me I can't help falling in love with you."

No thanks. She would wonder if he'd gone crazy. But then things happened to Adam at work, funny things, terrible things, bizarre things and he had no one to tell them to, no one to share them with but Elvis, and he found himself missing Mandy even more. Elvis's company left something to be desired.

There were days when he could hardly drag himself to work. One of those days he wished he hadn't. There, leaning against the door of Parvo Petrochemicals was a tall, scruffy-looking character in a plaid, flannel shirt, his hands in his pockets. Adam rocked back on his heels.

"What in the hell are you doing here?"

"Is that any way to greet your best friend?"

"Sorry, but I thought you would be planning your honeymoon with Miss Illinois," Adam said.

Jack shook his head. "It's a long story. Can we go in and talk? I've been waiting outside for an hour. What time do you start around here, anyway?"

Adam looked at his watch. "Eight or nine. Whenever I get here. You have a problem with that?" He knew he was being obnoxious, but he couldn't help it. Here was Jack, soon to be happily married, grinning like a cat who'd got the cream, come to rub it in.

"Not me," Jack said cheerfully. "You can come in at noon if you want." He followed Adam into the office. "So, how's Mandy?" Jack asked, taking the chair on the other side of the desk.

"That's a strange question for a man who's about to be married to someone else," Adam observed, stepping around his friend to get to his desk.

"That's what I have to talk to you about. It's all off."

"What?" Adam sat down hard in his padded office chair.

Jack scratched his head. "Everything was fine until we got to Illinois. Then, I don't know why, but it all fell apart."

"When you told her you weren't a millionaire?"

"That's the funny thing. My mine is producing. I *am* a millionaire, or I will be as soon as I get my check. I sold out to a consortium up there. Now what do you think?" he demanded with a broad smile.

Adam rocked back in his swivel chair until the back of his head hit the wall with a thud. "I'm speechless."

"Is that why you didn't answer my question?"

"I don't know how Mandy is," Adam said brusquely. Then he narrowed his gaze. "Why?"

"You know why. You told me I had to see her, you said she was the one. Kind, caring, warm, sensitive, eight on a scale of one to ten," Jack prodded.

"I said that?" Adam asked, stalling for time. He had to keep Jack from seeing that Mandy was a ten-plus, from throwing himself and his million dollars at her. Why? Because it wasn't fair. To whom? To Mandy, of course. Mandy, who was on the rebound from Jack and who just might rebound right *back* to Jack. He had a duty to protect Mandy from Jack, who was bouncing from one woman to another like a rubber ball.

"You said that. How far away is her place from here?" Jack asked, propping his feet on Adam's desk.

Adam frowned, wondering if he could say the road was impassable, and the coast was cut off from the rest of the world. "Not far," he said at last. "But she may not be there. She may be . . . out somewhere."

"There's only one way to find out." Jack swung his legs down from the desk and lunged for Adam's telephone.

Adam watched while his friend dug a small address book from his shirt pocket and then dialed her number. She wouldn't be there, Adam hoped, and she wasn't. But he was forced to listen while Jack left a lengthy message telling her who he was and that he was on his way over there to see her. Adam bored holes through Jack with his eyes, but it didn't do any good, he just kept talking. On *his* phone. In *his* office. Finally, he reminded Jack in a hoarse whisper that he had work to do and business calls to make. Jack wound up his message and hung up.

"Just because you don't have to work anymore..." Adam said, watching Jack walk to the coffee machine.

"It's a great feeling," Jack admitted, filling a cup. "You ought to try it. You seem tense and irritable. You need a vacation."

"I just had a vacation. Which I spent doing research for you."

"Which couldn't have been easy. I know. I owe you for that."

Adam shook his head. "Forget it," he said wearily.

"I won't forget it. We'll name our first child after you."

Adam snapped a No. 2 lead pencil in two.

"Well," Jack said, draining his coffee cup, "I guess I'l mosey on over to the Miramar Inn. I picked me up a map a the gas station and got directions just in case I couldn't find you." He patted the pocket of his shirt.

"Wait a minute," Adam interjected, "you didn't tell me what happened with Julie."

"I thought you had work to do."

"I do, but you said you wanted to talk about it."

"Not now. I don't want to keep Mandy waiting."

Adam watched helplessly as Jack went out the door and got into a shiny new red sports car. Short of throwing him self across the hood, Adam couldn't think of any way to stop him. He just stood there in the doorway, staring at the place where Jack's car had disappeared from view, feeling as if he was sinking into the icy waters of the North Sea.

The worst part was that it was his own fault. He was the one who had praised Mandy to Jack. And Jack to Mandy What would happen when Jack arrived at the Miramar Inn' Would Mandy come running to the door and fling out he arms in a warm welcome the way she'd done for Adam?

Would Jack help her wallpaper, get breakfast in bed, and take her sight-seeing? She'd be too busy for that, wouldn' she? Too busy to notice that Jack was a damn nice guy Adam didn't know why he'd been so short with him. He wa his best friend, an almost-millionaire, and all he needed to make his life complete was a wife. Mandy was available. She had a wonderful house and no one to share it with. Jack ha a million dollars but no house. They needed each other They deserved each other. And to stand in their way was the height of selfishness.

Adam was able to keep to that line of reasoning for three days, then he broke down and called the inn. It was te o'clock in the morning and instead of the answering machine, he reached Mandy herself. He sucked in a deep breath and forgot what he was going to say.

"How's everything?" he asked finally, bracing one hand on the edge of his desk.

"You won't believe who's here," she said breathlessly.

"The B52's?" he asked.

"No. Why, can you hear the music? I play it when I'm cleaning."

"Or wallpapering," he suggested.

"You remember," she said, sounding surprised and pleased.

I remember everything that happened there, everything about you, he wanted to say, but he didn't. "Who *is* there?" he asked. Might as well get it over with.

"Jack. Jack Larue from the Yukon."

He ground his teeth together. Still there, after three days? Well, what did he expect? Maybe he could change the subject, now before he heard any more disturbing news. But he was gripped with an insatiable curiosity. "Really?" he asked.

"Really. He didn't get married, after all. It fell through. You could have knocked me for a loop," she said with a little giggle.

"Me, too," he said grimly. "Is he, uh, staying with you?"

"Yes, in Laurie's room. I've been completely booked, you know, thanks to you."

"What do you think of him?" Adam asked, holding his breath.

"Um…what? Just a minute. Jack just woke up. I'd better get him some breakfast. Nice to hear from you, Adam."

"Nice to hear from you, too," he muttered after he'd hung up. What was going on there? Couldn't she have told him what she thought of Jack before she'd hung up? Not that it mattered. Objectively he'd have to say that Jack was a decent, good-looking guy with a million dollars—the kind of guy any woman would fall for.

But was Mandy just any woman? Adam got no work done that day, thinking about that. He finally went home and asked Elvis what he thought, but the bird was strangely noncommittal. The only advice he offered was not to step on his blue suede shoes.

"Elvis," Adam said, offering him a plum. "I know where you're coming from, but I've got to see them together before I leave. Then I can go to the North with peace of mind, knowing I've done the right thing. If I don't, I'll never know. I'll always wonder. So tomorrow I'll hang an out-to-lunch sign on the door and mosey on over to the Miramar Inn, as Jack would say. It won't take long. With my perception I'll know right away if they're right for each other. After all, I'm a scientist," he assured the colorful bird.

But the next day before he could even leave the house, Adam got a call from their installation in Saudi Arabia. There was an emergency and Adam had to go through the files and get on the phone. Afterward he threw a change of clothing in his leather overnight bag just in case, but it was five o'clock before he got away from the office.

On the way down the winding road, he prepared himself for the worst. He might not even go into the house. He might just look through the front window and if he saw them together he might just turn around and go home. After all, there was just so much a man could take.

But when he got there it was dark and Jack's red sports car was not out in front. There were two other cars parked there. Through the window he could see strangers drinking sherry and eating hors d'oeuvres. The house looked warm and inviting and Adam felt a tightening in his chest, a longing for the home he'd never had, the family he'd missed. If he leaned forward, he could even see Mandy's family pic tures on the wall. But neither Mandy nor Jack was anywhere in sight.

Adam opened the front door without knocking. The guests greeted him warmly, mistaking him for a fellow guest, no doubt. He asked for Mandy, they pointed to the kitchen. He opened the kitchen door to find the room filled with smoke and every surface covered with pots and pans. In the middle of the room Mandy was standing with a cleaver in her hand and an apron wrapped around her body. Her nose was red, tears were running down her face, and she looked absolutely beautiful.

In two seconds he'd crossed the room and stopped just short of crushing her to him and kissing away her tears. "What's wrong?" he asked hoarsely.

She looked up and gave him a watery smile. "Nothing," she said, "it's the onions. What are you doing here?"

He blanked out. His mind reeled. To say he was just in the neighborhood wouldn't be believable, and he couldn't say he was there to see Jack without admitting he knew him.

"Never mind," she said, wiping her eyes with the corner of her apron. "I'm trying to make that chicken dish you fixed. But I keep messing up. I should have paid more attention. The night when you...the night when I..." she trailed off.

He knew what she was going to say—the night when he'd kissed her, the night they'd eaten by candlelight. "I thought you didn't do dinners."

"I don't want to. But sometimes I have no choice. And I realize I've got to expand. I can't afford to turn anyone down. I thought I could make it, but so far all I've made is a mess." She paused and wiped a tear of frustration from her eye. "I'm glad to see you," she said softly. "Can you stay for dinner?" Then she looked around the kitchen and hiccuped loudly.

"You mean, can I stay to make dinner?"

She put her cleaver down and laid her hands on his shoulders. "I can't let you do that. Not again. Just sit down and keep me company. Keep me from going crazy."

"How many guests do you have?" he asked, picking up the cleaver and slicing an onion with a swift stroke.

"Four. Five, actually, counting Jack."

"Jack? Is he still here?"

She nodded, measuring rice into a cup.

"Where is he? Why isn't he helping you?"

She turned the stove on. "He's a guest," she explained patiently. "I sent him to the Seadrift for dinner."

Adam heated some oil in a pan. "Good. He'll like it."

"How do you know?"

"Just a feeling. How do you like him?"

"He's fine." She looked up at Adam for a moment. "I thought he'd be more like you," she said reflectively, her gaze lingering on the angle of his jaw, the way his hair slanted across his forehead.

"It must have been a pleasant surprise to find he wasn't," Adam said, throwing the onions into the pan.

Mandy laughed and he grinned at her. Their eyes locked and held, and Adam's grin faded. Mandy felt a pressure building inside her, a tingling in every nerve end. Adam filling the room with positive ions, filling her with a longing she couldn't deny. Her heartbeat accelerated every time he brushed by her on his way to the counter, every time he touched her hand when they traded utensils. He was everywhere, in the pantry, behind the stove, and he was bigger than she remembered, better-looking, more irresistible, more everything.

With Adam here she almost forgot about Jack. Adam lifted a spoonful of sauce for her to taste and she met his gaze as the rich, thick sauce touched her lips. For a long moment she couldn't move, couldn't swallow, couldn't think, could only feel the earth shake and the sky rumble

But there was no earthquake and no storm. There was only Adam. And that was enough.

"Well?" he asked.

"Wonderful." She sighed. "How do you do it?"

"You inspire me," he said, his eyes brimming with some emotion she couldn't understand.

She backed to the sink to rinse the lettuce. "I've missed you," she confessed, spraying water all over her apron.

"Even with Jack here?" he asked.

She bit her lower lip. "Even with Jack here," she confessed. If only Adam were more like Jack, or Jack more like Adam.

"Maybe you expected too much of him," Adam suggested.

She nodded. "I thought I knew him so well from his letters. But I feel like I don't know him at all. It's funny. Well, he'll be back soon and you can tell me what you think of him."

He turned back to the stove. "I might not have time to hang around. I've got to get back. Elvis hates to be alone too long."

"That's too bad. You two have a lot in common."

"Me and Elvis? Thanks."

She smiled and shook the excess moisture off the lettuce. "Jack wants to meet you," she said.

"I'll bet," Adam muttered. "Maybe some other day. Is he still looking for a wife?"

Mandy felt a flush creep up her face. "I don't know."

He turned to face her. "He could be the right person for you."

"I don't think so," she said softly.

"Why not?" He outlined the edge of her apron with his fingers, burning a trail along the top then the sides of her breasts.

She held perfectly still, while the meat sizzled in the pan behind her. She was aching to have him hold her, to feel his body against hers. She should be watching the pot, but it might be the last time, the last time she saw him, the last kiss. She tilted her head and his lips met hers, warm, firm and demanding. She was flooded with desire, a pounding need she couldn't explain or deny.

His fingers fumbled with her apron ties, the apron fell to the floor. His hands spanned her ribs and cupped the warm fullness of her breasts through her soft cotton shirt.

She was on fire. She wanted nothing more than to tear off her clothes and his, too, to lead him to her room and let the world go on without them. But she couldn't. There were guests and dinner. She broke away. She was breathing hard and so was he. He stared at her for a long moment, then shook his head.

"I'll serve the salad," she said.

"Wait." He turned her around by the shoulders so her back was to him. Then he swiped the apron from the floor and tied it around her waist. Next he lifted the curls that brushed her shoulders and kissed the back of her neck. The scent of her hair brought back memories and all he wanted was to carry her up to the bedroom where he'd once slept, where she'd served him breakfast in bed, and make love to her all night long while the waves pounded the shore below and the salt air drifted in the windows.

But there was someone else in that room now. He'd missed his chance. It was gone, over, done with. He'd had his opportunity, before Jack, before his boss had claimed him, and he'd blown it. He watched her go into the dining room and he was filled with an unbearable sadness, as if he might never see her again, even though he knew she'd be back in a moment. He shouldn't have come. He couldn't handle these ups and downs anymore.

But somehow he got through the dinner. When it was over and the dishes were done, Mandy collapsed on the couch in the living room and Adam stood at the front door. If he left now, he might miss Jack. But if he left now, he'd have to say goodbye to Mandy forever. He gripped the door handle and someone turned it from the outside.

Jack walked in the door and stared openmouthed at Adam. Adam grabbed his hand and shook it. "You must be Jack," he said loudly, with a meaningful edge to his voice.

Jack nodded, then looked at Mandy. "Friend of yours?" he asked.

Mandy nodded. "Jack, this is Adam. You two have a lot in common."

"More than you know," Jack muttered.

"I was just leaving," Adam said.

"So soon?" Jack asked, holding the door open for him.

Adam's eyes narrowed. It made sense to leave now. But seeing Mandy ensconced on the couch, her gaze drifting between himself and Jack, he couldn't do it. Not until he got some sense of what, if anything, was going on.

"Don't go," Mandy said, and that cinched it. He closed the front door and leaned back against it. Jack took the chair next to the fireplace and stretched his legs out in front of him. He looked so comfortable Adam wanted to strangle him.

"Right," Jack said with a grin. "Don't go. Not yet. What brings you over this way?"

"Adam actually cooked the dinner tonight," Mandy explained.

"Really? I'll bet he's a good cook. I'll bet he's just about the best chef in the Arctic Circle."

"That's right!" Mandy agreed. "How did you know?"

"It's a small world. I've heard of him." He turned to Adam. "What did you say you were doing here?"

"Just checking in on Mandy, making sure she's all right."

"She looks all right to me," Jack said. "In fact, she looks just about perfect." Jack shot Mandy an appreciative glance that Adam didn't appreciate at all. In fact, it made him feel sick.

"If you two will excuse me," Mandy said suddenly, rising from the couch, "I'm going to bed. It's been a long day and I'll leave you to reminisce about the Yukon. Help yourselves to some sherry." And with a polite smile she went down the hall to her bedroom.

Adam stared after her, realizing he hadn't said goodbye, knowing he'd never say goodbye now.

Jack brought him back to reality. "At the risk of sounding repetitious, what are you doing here, old buddy?"

"I told you," Adam said. "I came to check up on Mandy."

"Mandy's fine. I could have told you that."

"She wasn't fine when I got here. She was overwhelmed and overworked. Where were you when she needed somebody?" Adam stalked to the sideboard and poured himself a glass of sherry.

Jack studied his friend for a long moment. "You really like her, don't you?"

"Of course I like her, don't you?" Adam demanded. "Because if you don't, tell her now. I don't want her hurt again."

"*You* don't want her hurt? What are you, her guardian angel?"

"I'm her friend, that's all."

"I don't think that's all," Jack said. "And isn't it about time to tell her the truth?"

Adam sat on the arm of the couch. "The truth, from the beginning? How you lied about being a millionaire, how I wrote the letters, how I came down here to spy on her? Are you crazy?" he demanded in a loud whisper.

"Maybe," Jack admitted, "but what's the alternative?"

"The alternative," Adam said, draining his glass, "is for you to marry Mandy and live happily ever after. She doesn't need to know how it really happened. She just needs someone to love her, to help her, to give her back the confidence she lost when she got dumped the last time."

Jack angled his head for a different view of his friend. "I don't see it that way. I see her as a woman who's got love to give, who can give a man the confidence he needs. I see her as the woman I described in my ad, warm, sensuous, understanding, with good math skills to boot."

"Of course. I know that."

"Then quit trying to protect her. She's not a charity case. She'll find someone without you helping her."

"Who, you?"

"I don't think so."

Adam jumped to his feet. "Why not? What's wrong with her? What's wrong with you?"

"I don't know what's wrong with me, but I know what's wrong with her, she's in love with someone else."

"There is no one else," Adam insisted.

Jack shook his head wearily. "Okay, okay. I admit I don't know anything about love and marriage. If I did, I'd be happily married by now. But I know one thing, you can't have a relationship based on lies. So if you don't tell Mandy the truth, I will."

Adam's heart pounded. "You can't. You won't."

"I can. I will," Jack said. "Unless you do."

Adam forced himself to stand straight, to give the blood a chance to return to his heart and circulate through his body. He couldn't do it, couldn't tell her, couldn't stand to hurt her. But he couldn't stand to have Jack tell her, either.

"Okay," he said at last. "I'll tell her, and then you can ask her to marry you."

"I already did."

Adam staggered backward and narrowly missed crashing into the coffee table. *"What?"*

"She turned me down."

"I don't believe you. You should have seen her face when she got your letter. She's in love with you."

"Guess not."

"When was this . . . proposal?"

"Last night. I took her to the Seadrift, plied her with food and wine, and then I asked her."

Adam sank into the cushions of the couch. "Are you saying she turned you down?"

"How do you think I feel? A few weeks ago I had a hundred prospects. Now I have none. Where did I go wrong? I've got a million dollars and no hang-ups like you do about the challenge of the Yukon or the dangers of marriage— nothing to prove. I'm free to live wherever I want. I love kids. I help old people across the street, and I'm sensitive and caring. The ultimate nineties man. But does it do me any good? Has it got me a wife?" Jack hunkered down into the depths of the big, stuffed chair and closed his eyes.

For the first time that night Adam looked at his friend with sympathy. He'd been so immersed in his own misery, it hadn't occurred to him that Jack might be suffering, too. He felt like a self-centered jerk. If Jack was a man for the nineties, then Adam was stuck in the seventies, the selfish, me generation.

"I'm sorry," Adam muttered.

Jack waved his hand in dismissal. "No hard feelings. But before you go, I've got something for you."

Adam followed him out the front door to the red sports car. Jack reached into the back seat and handed him a cardboard box.

"What's this?"

"Mandy's letters. You wrote to her. They're yours now."

"But I don't . . . I'm not . . ."

Jack didn't let him continue. He shook hands with Adam and then he went back inside the house without another word. Adam stood in front of the house for a long time, listening to the sound of the sea in the distance, holding the box of letters in his hands until his fingers were numb. Then he drove home to the big house with the noisy, cantankerous bird, wishing he'd never written to Mandy. He wished he had never answered a single letter so Jack would have answered them.

Life was so simple before she'd come into his life, so simple and so empty. Maybe she felt the same way about him. Maybe she wished he'd never come into her life, either. If she didn't now, she would as soon as she heard the truth. When would that be? It had to be soon, but he wasn't looking forward to it.

Chapter Nine

Laurie Clayton stood in the middle of the kitchen floor with her hands on her slim hips. "You did what?" she asked her sister, who was removing a tray of blueberry muffins from the oven.

"I turned him down," Mandy said calmly.

"An honest-to-goodness millionaire, whom you've come to know and respect through countless letters, appears in person and asks you to marry him and you turn him down?" Her normally well-modulated voice was dangerously close to a shriek. "What was wrong with him?"

"Nothing. I just don't love him."

"You don't love him. How could you tell? He was only here a few days. Besides, marrying for love is vastly overrated. There are no guarantees that love will last. But a million dollars lasts a long time if you invest it properly. Did you give the poor guy a chance?"

"I think so. Sit down and try one of these."

"I can't. I'm too upset. Let me get this straight. There are two men in your life, right? And they're both from the Yukon."

"Wrong. There are no men in my life, from the Yukon or anywhere else." Mandy pulled out a chair and sat down at the table. She removed a muffin from the tin and held it up. "What do you think, tall enough?"

Laurie whirled on her heels. "Tall enough? The man was over six feet, and . . . oh, you mean the muffin."

Mandy smiled in spite of her heavy heart. "Honestly, you have a one-track mind. There are other things in the world besides men. If there weren't, I'd be in bad shape."

Laurie crossed her arms over her chest. "But you're in good shape, excellent shape, which is why all these men are beating a path to your door. Don't tell me you think it's because of your blueberry muffins?"

"As you know, the vast majority of my visitors are couples who have yet to notice my shape or anything about me. They come for the view, the romantic atmosphere, and maybe even for my outstanding muffins, which you haven't even tried."

"Which one do you like best?" Laurie asked.

"That's what I was going to ask you," Mandy explained.

Laurie narrowed her eyes. "Well, I didn't see Jack, but I thought Adam was awfully cute. On the other hand, he's not as rich as Jack and that has got to be a factor."

Mandy shook her head in dismay. "I was talking about the muffins. Whether you like bran or blueberry better. Do you ever think about anything but men?"

"Don't tell me you don't think about men. Don't tell me you weren't interested in Adam. And don't tell me there wasn't something going on between you two." Laurie took the chair on the other side of the table and propped her elbows on the table. "There was so much electricity in the air that night I was afraid of getting singed. And what about the next morning, the grass stains on your pants and on his? How do you explain those?''

''You want me to explain the grass stains?'' Mandy asked as if she'd been asked to explain the theory of relativity.

''If you can.''

Mandy threw up her hands. ''All right. Adam and I had a picnic in the Napa Valley, where there are rolling hills covered with grass.''

Laurie sighed loudly. ''If you won't admit to me how you feel about him, then you're not admitting it to yourself. But I think the reason you turned Jack down has something to do with how you feel about Adam.''

''There's no point in discussing this any further,'' Mandy said, brushing the crumbs off her lap. Laurie was just too perceptive. ''Because Adam has gone back to the Yukon for good and Jack has gone off to find someone to marry. So it's all over, finished and done with.''

Mandy stared out the window at the rain clouds hovering over the ocean. It was hard enough to get her mind off Adam without Laurie's penetrating questions. She had a permanent ache in the vicinity of her heart every time she thought about Adam leaving without saying goodbye. She'd heard their voices like a low rumble in the living room that night, but she hadn't been able to make out a single word.

In the morning Adam had been gone and Jack had asked her to reconsider his offer. But she hadn't needed to. She knew Jack wasn't the man for her. Even after all those wonderful letters. She went to the sink to soak the empty muffin pans and blink back the tears that sprang to her eyes. She didn't know what she'd do without her sister there to keep up a brave front for. If it weren't for Laurie and the constant stream of guests, Mandy would probably sit in front of the fire and wallow in self-pity all day long.

After Laurie left for the airport that afternoon, and the rain pelted her windows, Mandy reached into her closet and pulled out a stack of letters tied with a ribbon. There on the couch with a fire crackling in the fireplace she was determined to put an end to self-pity and unrealistic dreams once and for all.

Today she would burn all of Jack's letters and start a new life. A life without Adam or Jack. Because Laurie was right, she'd gone off the deep end over Adam. And yet she hardly knew him. It wasn't as if she'd corresponded with *him* for six months. He came, they met, and she lost her head. Her heart, too. But it wasn't love. It couldn't be love. It had to be lust. And she could get over lust. Just as soon as she got rid of those letters.

If it hadn't been for Adam, she might have considered Jack, but now she couldn't. She wanted it all, love and lust and laughter—the whole thing.

She tucked her legs underneath her, leaned back against the cushions, and started at the beginning with Jack's first letter. It took all afternoon, but she reread every letter. She laughed and cried as she read about Jack's experiences digging for oil, about the people he met and his thoughts on everything under the sun.

Toward the end, his letters got personal, telling her how much he wanted to meet her in person, his plans and hopes for the future. How he wanted to leave the Yukon, settle down and get married. Her tears flowed freely now, blotting the words and smudging the paper. Mandy blew her nose carefully and put the letters back in a neat stack. She stood in front of the fire, but she couldn't do it. She couldn't throw them into the flames.

She wasn't strong enough. Not yet. She was still a sentimental idiot, daydreaming about someone who didn't exist except in her imagination.

She was putting the letters back in the closet when the telephone rang. "Miramar Inn," she said as cheerfully as she could, given her state of mind.

"Hello, Mandy."

"Adam." She grabbed a chair to sit down before she fell down. "I thought you'd be..."

"I'm on my way to the North Sea, finally."

"That's wonderful. You must be very happy."

"I thought I'd drop by to say goodbye."

"Oh, that's not necessary. Couldn't we just say goodbye on the phone?" she asked desperately. That was all she needed was to see Adam again, to hear how excited he was to be leaving, how much he was looking forward to his new life while she pretended to wish him well. No, she couldn't do it.

"I'd rather come by. I've got something to tell you."

"Why don't you tell me over the phone?"

"I can't. Will you be home this afternoon?"

"Not really. I'm... I'm going to be out... gathering mussels on the beach." There, it was believable and it was true. It was mussel season and he knew it.

"I'll help you."

"I only have one bucket."

"I'll bring my own," he insisted.

"It's raining."

"I'll wear my hip boots. It won't take long, I promise. I'll be there in an hour."

Mandy stared at the phone in her hand. Adam had hung up on her. He was coming over. What was she going to do?

Adam hung up before she could think of another reason to stop him. He didn't blame her for not wanting to see him and this was not an encounter he was looking forward to. But he'd promised Jack and he'd promised himself. He found a bucket in Gene's basement and called himself every kind of coward for not telling her before. And for not getting rid of her letters.

He'd never get over her until he got rid of them. But instead, he read them over and over, reliving the excitement he'd felt when they'd come in the mail. Reading them, he felt as if he'd known her forever, loved her even longer. He dropped his bucket on the cement floor. *He'd fallen in love with Mandy by mail and he'd never known it until now.* Not that it mattered. Not that it changed anything. It just made it more imperative that he get out of there so she could find someone better, someone who wouldn't love her and leave her.

Jack was right. Mandy had so much to give. She was warm, sensuous and understanding. She understood why he had to work on a drilling platform. She might even understand why he'd lied to her, why he'd pretended to be someone he wasn't. She might, but he doubted it.

He clomped up the basement stairs in his high-top boots and took off on the road to the coast and Mandy. An hour later he was peering into her house through the front window, but there were no lights on, and only embers in the fireplace. Still the room reflected Mandy's warmth and charm, with its hand-woven rug on the floor and the candles on the mantel.

It was a house that welcomed weary travelers, whether they came from the other side of the bay or the other side of the world. It was a house that said, "Let me be your home away from home, or if you have no home, I'll take you in." He'd never forget the first day he'd rung the bell and she had come to the door covered with wallpaper paste, her arms outstretched so wide he'd almost walked into them.

If he'd known then what he knew now... what would he have done? Turned around and walked away before it was too late? It wasn't too late now. He could leave a note telling her he was sorry. But that wouldn't do. He had to tell her in person.

He made his way to the back of the house to the wooden steps that led to the beach, swinging his bucket in his hand. The rain had let up, but the fog was so thick at ground level he couldn't see the bottom of the steps. He shouted her name, but his voice was swallowed up in the damp grayness. What if he never found her? What if she'd been swept out to sea? At the bottom of the steps he dropped his bucket and ran down the beach, yelling her name. But his cries blended with the cries of the gulls overhead. He spun around and retraced his steps and crashed into her, sending her bucket of mussels flying across the sand.

He grabbed her by the arms and crushed her to him, shiny slicker, hat and all. She smelled like sea salt and brine and her soap, the essence of summer berries. "Where were you?" he demanded, his mouth against her cheek.

"On the rocks," she said breathlessly, brushing his jacket off. "Watch out, I'm slimy."

"You're slimy? Oh, Mandy."

She bent over to retrieve the lost mussels. "What is it you want to tell me?"

"Could we sit down?" he asked.

She nodded in the direction of a large rock jutting out behind them. He wedged himself against the rock, feeling the dampness creep in through his denim jeans. For the life of him, he couldn't think of how to begin. Not with her leaning on the rock next to him, staring straight ahead.

"So, you're leaving soon," she said when it appeared he wasn't going to say anything.

"Yes, we finally have things settled at the office."

"Your boss got better?"

"Much better, and his ex-wife moved back in to take care of him."

"That's good. Maybe they'll get back together again."

"Looks like it," he said.

"So there are happy endings, after all," she noted.

"For some people." Another silence.

Tell her, tell her now. It isn't going to get any easier, urged is inner voice.

"How's Elvis?" she asked.

"Fine. He said to tell you hello. Actually, he said he was othing but a hound dog. Bet you didn't know that." Out f the corner of his eye he studied her face, her cheeks rned ruddy from the cold, her hair in a mass of tight curls om the damp air. He wished he could bury his face in her ft ringlets, sweep her off her feet and carry her to her ouse. Her warm, welcoming house that beckoned to him, at seemed more like home than any home he'd ever had.

"What did you think of Jack?" she asked.

"Jack?" he repeated.

Yes, Jack. The guy you've known for ten years, known so ell you write his letters for him, the voice chided nastily.

"He seemed nice. What did you think?" he asked.

"I thought he was nice, too."

"But not nice enough to marry?" he asked.

Her eyes swerved in his direction. "He told you that?"

"We were talking about you and he mentioned it. He ems like a good guy. He's got money and no obligations. remember all the good things you said about him before he ot here. What happened?"

She didn't say anything.

"There's no one else, is there?" he prodded.

She nudged her half-full bucket with the toe of her boot. No, no one else. Does there have to be? Can't someone rn someone down just because?"

"Don't you want to get married?" he asked.

"No, I don't. I've got everything I need. A thriving busi- ess and complete freedom to do whatever I want when I ant to. You of all people should understand that. Imagine how you'd feel if you had a wife to whom you needed to explain why you were going off to work on a drilling platform. You'd feel guilty, and she'd feel lonely."

"And she'd leave," he said.

She put her hand on his arm and he drew back. He didn't want her sympathy, not now. "Mandy," he said abruptly, "Jack and I are old friends. We've worked together in the Yukon for years drilling for oil."

She turned slowly to face him. The blood had drained from her face. Even her lips were white. "What?"

"He advertised for a wife in *Yukon Man*. I wrote the letters for him."

"You...did...what?"

"I wrote the letters. Not all of them. But most of them. He couldn't keep up. I wanted to help him." Oh, God, his excuses sounded so lame in his ears, so inexcusable.

"You wrote all of the letters, to all of the women?" she asked slowly, unable to take it all in.

"I wrote *some* of the letters to all of the women. I wrote all of the letters to you."

She shook her head and tiny drops of water spilled over her forehead and collected in her eyelashes. "Why?"

"Why?" He gazed out at the waves that crashed against the shore. It was time to be honest with her and with himself. "Because I liked the way you sounded. I liked what you said about yourself. You interested me. You intrigued me. I wanted to hear more about you."

"But this wasn't about you. This was about Jack."

"I know. I was doing it for Jack."

Liar, you were doing it for yourself. "I was trying to find the right person for him. I thought it was you."

"You were wrong," she said icily.

"I know that now." He looked longingly up at the cliff above them, wondering if he should have thrown himself off it. Then at least she'd have happy memories of him. Now she'd have nothing but bitterness every time she thought of him. If she ever thought of him. The cold crept into his leather jacket, and through his sweater and into his bones. Mandy's profile was so white and so still it might have been carved out of marble. With every word he spoke, he felt as if he was driving a stake into her heart.

"Why did you lie when I asked if you knew Jack?" she asked, her voice as cold as the west wind that blew off the ocean.

"I would have blown the whole thing."

"I suppose you came to see if I was good enough for Jack."

"Yes."

"Obviously you decided I wasn't." A wave of helpless fury engulfed her. She squeezed her hands into fists and beat against his chest.

He grabbed her by the wrists, but she jerked away. "I thought you were good enough for him, I think you're good enough for anybody," he said through clenched teeth.

"Except you," she said, glaring at him with ice blue eyes.

"That's not true. You're too good for me." It was true, but it didn't stop him from wanting her.

"It doesn't matter," Mandy said wearily, dropping her arms to her sides. All the fight and the fury had gone out of her, leaving her feeling dead and cold inside. Nothing mattered except that she'd been set up and had fallen like a log for Adam. All that agonizing and worrying for nothing.

"It does matter," he protested. "It matters what I think of you and what you think of yourself."

"I don't care what you think of me," she said coldly. "Anyone who would lead me on for the purpose of spying on me doesn't deserve my concern."

"Leading you on was not part of the plan. It was something that just happened."

Mandy choked back the tears. Just something that happened? Just something that had happened to him while she was falling in love with him, falling in love with a man who didn't exist. "So the whole thing was a hoax from the beginning. I thought I was writing to a millionaire who was looking for a wife."

"You were. Jack is a millionaire who wants to get married. Technically, you were writing to him."

"Technically? Did he even read my letters?"

"I read them to him. Wait a minute." He took her arm and turned her to face him. "If you're not interested in money or in getting married, why did you write to Jack in the first place?"

Some of the color came back into her face. "Laurie dared me to and I've never refused a dare. And I felt sorry for him, alone and lonely in the Yukon. I didn't know he had you and the letters of hundreds of other women. I don't need to tell you I wish I'd never seen that stupid magazine. I wish I'd never listened to my sister."

"Wait a minute." He dropped her arm and smoothed her damp hair. "Are you saying you have no happy memories, none at all?"

Mandy bit her tongue. She'd never admit she wouldn't forget the first time she saw him in his bomber jacket, standing at the door like the ultimate Yukon man, like a gift from the gods. He'd appeared on her doorstep, had cooked her dinner, brought her breakfast in bed, and given her a smile that had turned her inside out. He'd made her laugh and finally made her cry.

"Happy memories?" she asked. "Of who? Of you or of Jack? I don't know who you are anymore." A sob caught in her throat.

"Don't you, Mandy?" He brushed the drops off her face with his thumb. She didn't know if they were tears or fog or rain, she just knew she couldn't stand here so close to him without wanting his arms around her, without wanting to hear the words he would never say—that he loved her, that he'd give up the Yukon for her or take her with him. No matter what she thought of him, the warmth and strength of his body were like a magnet to her. She craved his touch, wanted him now as much as she ever had, despite what he'd done.

She picked up her bucket, disgusted with him and even more disgusted with herself. "You can go now. You've done your duty. You've confessed and it's all over. I'm not angry, not anymore. And I'm not hurt or disappointed. So you don't have to worry about me. I hope you don't think it meant anything to me, what went on between us. As you say, it was just something that happened." She shrugged and even managed a small smile, then she turned and started down the beach.

She had hoped he'd let her leave, but she heard his footsteps in the sand behind her. "I said I'd help you gather mussels," he yelled.

"I don't need you." She tossed the words over her shoulder.

"I know that," he muttered, "but I'm going to help you, anyway."

She waded knee-deep into the water to a big black rock where the mussels clung in clumps on the other side. Lying flat on top of the rock, she pried the mollusks from the rock with a small, sharp knife and tossed them into her bucket. Adam worked alongside her, not speaking. Suddenly she set her knife down on a rocky outcrop and pulled herself to a sitting position.

"When you were writing all those personal things to me, were you you or were you Jack?"

"Partly I was Jack. But mostly I was me. I told you things about myself I've never told anyone else. I looked forward to your letters, no—I *lived* for your letters. What I did wasn't right and I have no excuses. But I wouldn't trade your letters for anything,'' he added in a husky voice.

"You have them?" she asked as the wind whipped her hair against her cheek.

He nodded. ''Why, do you want them back?''

''No.'' She ran her hand over the wet, smooth rock. ''I feel so stupid. How could I have been so stupid?''

''You're not stupid,'' he said vehemently.

''Not stupid? All the things you said to me, all the questions you asked me, all the places you took me. You didn't need to do that. I would have told you whatever you wanted to know without your being…so nice.'' Her voice broke and she turned her head and let the salt spray dampen her clothes. It was nothing compared to the waves of self-pity that threatened to wash her away.

''Mandy,'' he said, edging closer to her on the rock. ''I came to spy on you, I admit that, but once I got here, everything changed. I… Seeing you…connecting a face to the letters, a body to the mind…wasn't what I thought it would be. I knew you belonged to Jack, but I wanted you for myself. I tried not to, because I have nothing to offer a woman, just ask my ex-wife. I can't ask anyone to share my life. Where I'm going, no woman can come. But that didn't stop me from wondering…from imagining… All I can say is that I'm sorry.''

She slid down the rock and landed on her feet in the sand. ''I think I've heard enough,'' she said, brushing off the seat of her pants. ''I'm going home.''

''About Jack,'' he said hastily before she could go. ''He's really a good guy. He blames me for messing things up for him. I thought maybe you and he…''

She shook her head and he heaved a sigh of relief. As much as he wanted Mandy to find happiness and Jack to find true love, he didn't know what he'd do if they found it together. He wasn't a saint. He was only a man and there was just so much a man could take. If he had to stand and stare at her much longer, to watch the drops that collected in her eyelashes spill down her cheeks, he wouldn't have the strength to leave.

"Don't worry about me," she said, her chin raised to the stubborn angle he'd seen before. "Just go or you'll miss your plane or whatever it is you're taking. And don't try to match me up with Jack or anyone else. Whatever you think of me, I'm capable of managing my own life." She swallowed hard and wished he'd leave now and disappear from her life forever.

Every minute he stayed she felt more like a charity case who needed handouts of love and affection. "I don't need you or *Yukon Man* to make my life complete. My life is just fine the way it is," she said emphatically.

But he still didn't leave. He continued to stand there with his brow furrowed, his eyes deep and filled with some combination of remorse and pity. What could she do to make him understand? How could she make him believe her? In the cool gray fog he looked like a shadow of the real Adam Gray.

"Please go," she said quietly. "I appreciate your coming by, but there was really no need. I understand what happened and I understand why it happened. But you could have explained it to me on the phone. Of course I was hurt for a moment, but not anymore. I'm fine, just fine." She was proud of the way she kept her voice steady, of the way she disguised her shaking hands by clutching the handle of her bucket. "I'll look at it as if it were a learning experience, if I look at it at all. In a few days I'll have forgotten all about it and I'm sure you will have, too."

"I won't forget you," he said, and his eyes flashed with certainty.

"Yes, you will," she insisted. "Once you get to your drilling platform you'll have too much on your mind to think about anyone. I saw those pictures of the Yukon. It's beautiful and it's fascinating."

He reached out and touched her cheek, the saddest look in his eyes she'd ever seen. "So are you," he said in a hoarse whisper so soft she wasn't sure she'd heard him. And then he was gone. He turned and walked away and disappeared into the fog, leaving the imprint of his hand on her cheek.

Mandy's knees gave way and she sat down on the wet sand and buried her face in her damp blue jeans and sobbed until she'd exhausted herself. She wasn't sure who she was crying for, the woman who'd loved and lost for the second time or the man who'd had to break the news to her.

Chapter Ten

Rich petroleum deposits lie under the waters off the North Sea. Portable drilling platforms dot the coast from Point Barrow to the border of Canada. The platforms operate in water more than one hundred feet deep and the men drill to depths of twenty thousand feet or more. The dangers are numerous: fires from fuel leaks, falling gear from hoists, icy surfaces that make any movement on the platform risky, and high winds that could damage the rig and sweep everyone into the icy waters below.

In addition to the derrick and drilling machinery, the platforms have sleeping and eating rooms for the crew, as well as offices for the geological engineers who analyze core samples to instruct the men where to dig. But some engineers prefer the raw winds, the slick decks and the noise of the drill to the confines of a small office inside. Especially when they have trouble keeping their minds on their work.

Take Adam Gray, for example. Although his work was waiting for him in his office, he was roaming the deck restlessly, scanning the turbulent sea and the slate gray sky as if the answer to his problems was out there somewhere instead of deep inside him.

He'd been there a number of weeks now. Ordinarily the schedule was two weeks on, one week off, but Adam had elected to stay on the platform nonstop and had taken no breaks for R and R. Adam had waited so long for this choice assignment, he wanted to experience every moment of heart-stopping danger, excitement and thrills. And although he wouldn't admit it to anybody, he was afraid to leave in case what he'd been looking for all these years wasn't to be found on a drilling platform.

That was the fear that kept him there. Even now, a week before Christmas, he had no plans to go anywhere. There was a camaraderie on the platform and the men in their insulated jumpsuits and hard hats shouted greetings to him as he made the rounds from the tower to the derrick. There was excitement in the air as the men looked forward to the Christmas vacation. Replacements from the Lower 48 would arrive for short-term duty so anyone who wanted to leave, could.

When he was a child, Adam and his father didn't make much of the holidays. They were often in some remote site like this one and a Norman Rockwell-style Christmas was not a part of Adam's childhood memories. But this year he occasionally thought about Christmas at a charming house on the Pacific Coast, which probably had a wreath on the door by now, beckoning the guests coming there to sample Mandy's muffins, her afternoon sherry and her warm welcome at the door.

He wondered what she thought about him now, if anything. She'd probably forgotten about him after what he'd done to her. It was better if she did. Better that she got on with her life the way he was getting on with his. No, not that way.

There must be a better way to get on with your life than trudging the confines of a drilling platform like a caged animal, looking out to sea for something that would never come. He went inside then, not to escape the wind and the below-zero temperature, but to escape the endless monotony.

He checked his mailbox and found a few bills but nothing more. He wondered where Jack was, wondered if he'd found a wife. He wondered if Gene's ex-wife was still with him. Why he was so concerned with his friends' marital status, he hadn't a clue. It was of absolutely no importance to him.

He went to his office and examined slides under a microscope, but all he could see were wavy lines that reminded him of the curtains blowing in Mandy's bedroom, which reminded him of the green silk nightgown she'd been wearing when he'd brought her breakfast in bed. Which reminded him... He leaned back in his chair and closed his eyes. This wasn't good, this obsession with Mandy. It was coming between him and his work, work that had always meant everything to him, had meant enough to ruin his first marriage.

He unlocked the file cabinet behind his desk, reached in the back of the bottom drawer and drew out a box of letters. Mandy's letters. Then he put them on the middle of his desk and stared at them, daring himself to read through them again. Just to see if he could do it without coming unglued. Each time he did it, it should get better. He should become more detached. But it didn't work that way. Each time he read them, it got worse. He slipped further into a deep pit of regret. He didn't know if he could read them again, revisit the past and torture himself any more. He'd come here to start fresh, make a new beginning, instead he was going backward, sliding back two steps for every one step he went forward.

Not that it showed. He hoped no one knew. He hoped no one guessed from the way he acted around the installation. He was cheerful. God, was he cheerful, making jokes, remembering everybody's name and where they were from, their backgrounds. As if they were family. That was how it always was. His father had made the drilling site their home.

Nothing wrong with that. If it was good enough for his father, it was good enough for him. He had exactly what he wanted, but not what he'd expected. He hadn't expected to suffer from the boredom and the sameness and the loneliness. He hadn't expected to miss Mandy so much it felt like a sharp ache in the middle of his chest. He hadn't known he would have to pay for his mistakes and that the price would be so high.

Mandy's image floated through his dreams at night and continued into his daydreams. The one woman in the world who never wanted to see him again was the woman he saw over and over, but only in his dreams. He lowered his head and rested it on the box of letters. He didn't need to read them again. He knew them all by heart.

Mandy was standing on top of the ladder with a star in her hands, putting the finishing touch on her Christmas tree. She had gotten it attached to the top branch when the doorbell rang. It was gratifying to know that the guests continued to come. So gratifying, she hardly ever gave a thought to the man who had started her on the road to success with his letter to the newspaper.

She scarcely ever thought about him anymore, sometimes only once a day, when the fog rolled in about five o'clock and she remembered the day on the beach when he'd told her the truth. She would have preferred being hit over the head with the flat spade she used to dig clams. It would have been less painful. A lump on the head would have been better than the empty hollow in the pit of her stomach and a throat so dry she could hardly swallow.

But the worst part had been coming face-to-face with the fact that she'd been naive and stupid. But what else could she think? She'd overlooked the most blatant clues to Adam's background. The questions he'd asked, the questions he hadn't answered. It was all there and she hadn't seen it. She'd been blinded by his good looks and his charm.

Adam must have wondered where her brain was. He must have been amazed at how easy it was to fool her. There were times during the past weeks when the humiliation had washed over her like a tidal wave and it had taken all her efforts to keep a smile on her face for her guests.

Standing on top of the ladder with the star beaming at her, she knew that the very worst part was finding out that Adam had never cared for her at all. He'd only been investigating her for his friend. He'd certainly thrown himself into his work. She'd say that for him.

Fortunately it was almost Christmas and she had so much to do, so much to look forward to. Laurie would be home in a few days and there would be guests staying in the guest rooms. She brushed the pine needles off her hands and ran for the door.

"Hi, Mandy." Jack Larue stood on the doormat holding a package under his arm and looking so tentative and uneasy that she opened the door wide and invited him in. Then she offered him a glass of hot mulled wine she'd made for her guests.

He sat in the chair next to the fireplace, looking at her out of the corner of his eye. She assumed he'd say what he'd come to say eventually, so she sat down across from him and waited. Funny, she wasn't angry with Jack for his part in the charade. Maybe it was because Jack hadn't hurt her feelings. Jack had followed through. He'd even asked her to marry him, even though he wasn't in love with her. He was a nice guy, rich, too, but . . . She had to admit it, Laurie was right. The only thing wrong with Jack was that he wasn't Adam.

"How've you been?" Mandy asked at last. "Are you . . . have you found a wife or a job?"

"Funny you should ask," Jack said, crossing his leg over his knee. "It turns out jobs are easier to find than wives. My old boss Gene called and asked if I'd fill in up on the North Sea for the guys who are coming home for Christmas."

Mandy looked up at him and he read the question in her eyes. "No, not Adam. Adam's staying there. Adam has no place to go."

Mandy pressed her lips together and hardened her heart. You mean, he has no place he *wants* to go, she wanted to add. She would not feel sorry for him, if he had no place to go it was his own fault. He was the one who had put his work first all these years.

"You haven't heard from him, have you?" Jack asked.

Mandy shook her head. "I don't expect to. We really have nothing more to say to each other."

"Too bad," Jack mused, leaning back in his chair and gazing into the fire.

"Not at all," Mandy assured him. "I'm sure Adam is more than satisfied with his life up there. After all, it's what he's always wanted, isn't it?"

Jack shrugged. "It's what he always *said* he wanted." He turned to Mandy. "What about you?"

"Me? I couldn't be happier. If I think about Adam at all, which I hardly ever do . . ." She crossed her fingers behind her back. "It's with . . ." Oh, God, what was it with—anger, sorrow, regret, disappointment? "Mild interest," she finished.

"That's all?" Jack asked, drawing his eyebrows together.

"Yes," she said firmly, and changed the subject so that Jack could tell her about his travels and his gold mine. She even went to the kitchen and brought back a fruitcake wrapped in cellophane and tied with a red ribbon.

He thanked her, then brought the subject back to Adam again. "I'm sorry for sending Adam down here to spy on you. It was all my idea, you know. Adam didn't want to do it..."

"If he didn't want to do it, why did he?" Mandy interrupted. "What did you do, twist his arm in a hammerlock? I can't believe Adam could be forced to do something he didn't want to do."

"But it's true. The guy is so generous, such a damned good friend..."

Mandy got to her feet and ran her hands through her hair. "Come on, Jack. I know what he is. I know what he did. He's unscrupulous. At least you were sincere. You were sincerely looking for a wife. Adam was just toying with me."

Jack narrowed his eyes. "I'm not sure about that."

"You weren't here, you didn't see him," Mandy insisted.

"No, but I can imagine." Jack got up from his chair and gave the package to Mandy with an awkward gesture. "I don't know if you'll want this, probably not, after what you just said, but I thought I'd bring it by and show it to you, anyway. Go ahead, open it."

Mandy ripped the flap of the padded envelope and pulled out an old, framed black-and-white photograph of a tall man and a small boy standing in front of an oil well in a desert somewhere. The boy's level gaze met hers with a self-assurance beyond his years. Mandy's heart stopped beating and her eyes smarted with tears as she recognized the smile and the confident set of his shoulders.

"Is it..." she choked.

"Adam and his dad. My boss found it in his office. They were old friends, Gene and Adam's father. Thought the world of him. A loner just like his son."

Mandy nodded, unable to tear her eyes away from the picture of the boy with the shock of dark hair slanted across his forehead, the father with his arm draped over the boy's shoulders. The affection between them was unmistakable.

Jack backed toward the door, the fruitcake under his arm, clearly uncomfortable with the emotion the photograph had provoked.

Mandy held the picture out. "Don't you want to take it to him?" she asked.

Jack shook his head. "No place to hang pictures up there. Besides, it's better you hold on to it for him until..."

"But I won't. I won't ever see him again."

"You never know," Jack said, and then he was gone, into the night, leaving her with the picture in her hands, staring at it until her guests descended for hot mulled wine and hors d'oeuvres.

Adam expected the short-term vacation replacements, but he didn't expect Jack to be one of them. Jack didn't work for the company anymore.

"How'd he talk you into coming?" Adam demanded over coffee in the mess hall.

Jack shrugged. "No place else to go. I thought I'd be married by now. But since I'm not, I wanted to let some lucky bastard go home to his wife and kids."

Adam smiled reluctantly. "You could start over again. Put in another ad."

"Would you help answer the letters?"

Adam looked up at him. "What do you think?"

"I didn't think so, but...hell, it didn't work out so badly, did it?"

"Oh, no. I just hurt the one woman in the world who didn't deserve it."

"Don't worry about her. She's doing fine."

"How do you know?" Adam asked.

"Stopped by to see her the other day. She sent you a fruitcake. It's in my duffel bag."

Adam's mouth fell open in surprise. "You're kidding. Go get it."

Jack gave him a mock salute and was back in minutes with the gift-wrapped cake. He watched while Adam carefully peeled back the wrapping and inhaled the scent of nuts and fruit and brandy with his eyes closed.

"What did she say?" Adam asked. "Did she . . . say anything about me?"

"Yes. She said you were despicable."

"Then why did she send me the fruitcake?"

Jack shrugged. "Don't ask me. I don't understand women. She probably made too many. Or maybe she's got mixed feelings about you. Maybe she's confused. Love and hate are very close to the same thing, you know."

Adam shook his head. "How did she look?"

"The same."

Adam nodded. The same curly hair framing her face, the same wide blue eyes brimming with laughter one minute and burning with passion the next. The hands that could set him on fire with just a touch or beat against his chest in helpless fury.

"Oh, she said something else," Jack said, refilling his coffee cup.

Adam fastened his eyes on Jack and drummed his fingers on the table, though he would have preferred grabbing his friend by the shoulders and shaking him until he'd spat out everything that had happened between them.

"She said she thought about you . . . with mild interest."

"Well I don't think about her at all," he insisted.

"Then I'll take the fruitcake," Jack suggested.

"You will not. She sent it to me, didn't she?"

"Then you'd better write and thank her."

"I don't know about that," Adam said.

"Want some help?" Jack offered.

"No, thanks."

Adam took the fruitcake to his quarters at the rear of the barracks. A single room was a luxury reserved for senior scientists which he had never appreciated as much as he did at that moment. How strange, after pouring his heart out nonstop to Mandy all those months in letters, that he should be stumped at the thought of a simple thank-you note. He started it four times and when he finally finished, he had filled the wastebasket full of crumpled stationery.

He reread the final copy.

Dear Mandy,
Thanks for the fruitcake. It looks great. I hope business is good at the inn. Life up here is pretty much as I expected and then some.

Adam thought about telling her he missed her, but he didn't. He thought about confessing that life was not as exciting as he'd expected, but why bother? He didn't want her to feel sorry for him.

He thought about telling her he thought about her all the time, but she probably wouldn't believe him. It *was* unbelievable, coming all this way only to wish he'd stayed where he was, only to wish he could start all over again with Mandy without any deception or lies between them. But it was too late for that. He should have told her the day he'd walked into her house, the day he'd seen her for the first time. Because he'd known, even then. He'd known that she was the one. His destiny.

He opened the fruitcake and let the fragrance fill the small room. Just this once he'd give in to the memories and remember the good times and pretend they still had a chance, pretend that she still cared about him. But when reality set in, he knew the most he could hope for was that she'd forgiven and forgotten him.

On Christmas Eve, Mandy placed little gifts under the tree for her guests and after they'd retired to their rooms upstairs, she and Laurie sat on the floor next to the tree and opened their presents from each other.

"Just what I wanted, new stationery. I love the flowers around the edge," Mandy enthused.

Laurie smiled. "Just in case you have someone to write to again."

Mandy shot her a warning look. "I won't. And you can cancel your subscription to *Yukon Man,* as far as I'm concerned. Don't you think I've learned my lesson? You don't seriously think I'd ever write to a stranger again, do you? After what happened?"

"What about a non-stranger, someone who's stuck on an oil-drilling platform in the North Sea?"

Mandy set the box of notepaper down in front of her. "Nobody's 'stuck' anywhere," she explained patiently. "Anyone who's working on an oil rig is there for a reason. Because he's fulfilling some dream, or to make money, or to relieve one of the workers so he can come home for Christmas, like Jack."

"Jack sounds like a prince charming," Laurie commented.

"Yes, he is, and he's still available."

"So?"

Mandy shook her head. "Jack's a sweet guy, a great guy, for someone else. Jack never would have done what Adam did to me. No one would have." Mandy smoothed a wrinkle in her long, wool skirt, wishing she could smooth away the hurt and ache in her heart as easily.

"What did he do that was so terrible?" Laurie asked.

Mandy gave her sister an exasperated look. "I've told you before, about a thousand times before. This is the last—the absolute last—time I'm going to mention his name. As far as I'm concerned, he's out of sight and out of my mind. Gone, disappeared from my life forever. Have you got that?"

Laurie held up her hands. "I've got it. Just indulge me one more time and I promise I'll never mention him again."

Mandy took a deep breath. "First, he lied to me about not knowing Jack. Then he asked a lot of questions to find out if I was good enough for Jack."

"Disgusting," Laurie agreed.

"Exactly," Mandy agreed. "And then he decided I wasn't."

"Are you sure?"

"What do you think? Jack went off immediately to marry the other woman."

"But you're not interested in Jack. So what do you care?"

"I was at the time," Mandy explained.

"When I was here," Laurie mused, "I had the distinct impression that you were interested in Adam, and vice versa."

"Adam is an attractive man," Mandy said defensively.

"No kidding," Laurie agreed. "He's also funny, sexy, and he does dishes."

Mandy wanted to add that he did many other things, too, but she didn't dare. When Laurie was on a kick like this, she didn't need any more ammunition to fuel her fires. "Do you think I don't know all this?" Mandy asked. "Do you think it makes me feel any better to know how nice he can be when I also know what a rotten, deceiving—" Mandy stopped abruptly and took a deep breath. "But the worst part was that he wrote all those letters, the ones that supposedly came from Jack. Jack, the man who really wants to get married, who's honest enough to admit it and to go after what he wants."

Laurie wrapped a strand of tinsel around a branch of the tree. "So, you're mad because you fell in love with Adam by mail, thinking he was Jack. Then you fell in love with Adam all over again in person, not knowing he was really Jack."

"Yes, no . . . I don't know." Mandy got up and walked to the window. "I didn't fall in love with Adam or anybody. In the first place, nobody falls in love by mail."

"What about Elizabeth Barrett and Robert Browning?" Laurie asked.

"All right. Some people fall in love by mail, but I don't." Mandy looked longingly at the hall that led to her bedroom. When Laurie got started on one of these discussions she was like a terrier with a bone. She just wouldn't let go. Her miserable record with men was the last thing Mandy wanted to talk about on Christmas Eve, or ever. But Laurie had a theory that you couldn't put things behind you until you'd talked them out, over and over and over.

"You said Jack stopped by," Laurie commented.

"Yes, I gave him a fruitcake."

"What did he give you?"

"A photograph of Adam with his father. Taken years ago. I don't know why he gave it to me." She yawned deliberately. "I don't know about you, but I'm going to bed now. We've got to stuff that turkey in the morning, you know."

When Mandy finally escaped the all-seeing, all-knowing eyes of her sister, she closed the bedroom door behind her and took out the picture of Adam from her dresser drawer. Then she undressed and slipped into bed and propped the picture up against her knees. She wished she hadn't accepted it, wished she'd never seen Adam as a young boy or gained any insight into his childhood.

She didn't want to think about his parents splitting up or fighting over him. She didn't want to imagine him moving from place to place as he was doing now. She didn't want to understand him or care about him. It was too painful. Laurie was wrong. She wasn't mad. She was sad, so sad that she was close to tears at any given moment thinking of the man who'd turned his back on her and walked out of her life. He had never been half as interested in her as she was in him. That was the part that was hard to bear. She fell asleep clutching the picture in her hands, dreaming of Christmas in faraway places.

New Year's Eve on a drilling platform is not quite the festive occasion it is elsewhere. There was music, but it was in the form of golden oldies piped through the sound system that only contributed to the melancholy atmosphere that hung over the installation. There was only a skeleton staff on duty until the next day when most of the crew came back. Adam and Jack were in the mess hall after dinner each nursing a bottle of beer.

"I hate to leave you like this," Jack said, slapping Adam on the shoulder.

"Why?"

"Because you're not happy."

"How do you figure?" Adam asked, not pleased to know it showed.

"You haven't laughed at any of my jokes, you walk around in a fog, and you've been the first one at mail call this week. Who are you waiting to hear from?"

"I don't know. Gene, maybe."

Jack shook his head. "You didn't let me see your thank you letter to Mandy. Too personal?"

"Right," Adam said dryly.

Jack pulled a copy of *Yukon Man* out of his pocket. "Have you seen the latest issue?" he asked.

Adam shielded his eyes. "Put that thing away."

"I thought you'd want to see my new ad... and Mandy's."

Adam grabbed it out of Jack's hands. "Where?" He thumbed through the magazine until he came to a pen-and-ink sketch of a slope-roofed house on the edge of a cliff framed by cypress trees. "Miramar Inn," the copy read. "Your home away from home on the California Coast. Your hostess, Mandy Clayton." He stared at the ad, thinking of all the men who would go there, eat her muffins and share her patio, run on her beach and drink sherry in her living room. His heart contracted. If only... if only he could go there now, wipe the slate clean and start all over again. But that wasn't possible. He'd seen the hurt in her eyes when he'd confessed, and he'd heard the painful catch in her voice when she'd tried to act as if it didn't matter.

"Page forty-three."

Adam looked up and remembered where he was. "What?"

"My ad. Page forty-three."

Adam found it immediately. A large photo of Jack grinned engagingly at the reader with a list of his qualifications under the picture. Surprisingly, there was no mention of his being a millionaire. He looked at Jack, then back at the picture. "Not bad," he admitted. "But are you sure you want to go through this again?"

"I haven't given up," Jack said. "And neither should you. Come on, give it another try."

"Put an ad in *Yukon Man*?" Adam asked incredulously.

"Why not?"

"Mandy might see it."

"That's the idea," Jack said.

"I'll miss you, Jack," Adam said. "You're right. Yo
never give up." But Adam took the magazine and stuffed i
into his back pocket, while Jack watched with a smug look
on his face.

Jack left the next day, but the idea of putting an ad in
Yukon Man hung around long after Jack's departure. Every
time Adam walked into his cabin, the smell of brandy and
spices from the fruitcake haunted him along with the mag
azine. What if he put in a small ad, targeted for one person
only? And what if that one person saw it and answered it?

The worst that could happen was if she didn't see it and
didn't answer it. No, it would be worse if she saw it and *ther*
didn't answer it. Or she might write him a seething, scath
ing letter telling him how much she still despised him. But
even that would be better than nothing. Better than no
knowing if she was dead or alive, married or not married
She hadn't answered his thank-you note. He didn't think she
would. But she'd sent the fruitcake. You don't send fruit
cakes to people you hate, do you?

Normally Mandy put Laurie's mail in a basket and left i
in her room until she got back from a trip. But that day she
opened Laurie's issue of *Yukon Man* to see if they had got
ten her ad for the inn right. Then she riffled restlessly pas
well-toned loggers and fishermen with stocking caps an
sexy smiles. Halfway through, she stopped abruptly an
gripped the page between her thumb and forefinger. Ther
it was, in small print.

LONELY MILLIONAIRE seeks warm, sensuous
woman with bed and breakfast on the coast of California for long-term relationship. No math skills necessary, just a forgiving nature and the desire to start
over. I've made mistakes, but I've learned a few things
along the way....

Mandy fell into her desk chair and pressed her cool hands ainst her flaming cheeks. She hadn't answered his thank-ou note. What was there to say? I never sent you a fruit-ke? But this, this was different. The thing that worried her as his advertising himself as a millionaire. Did he think she as attracted to money? Did he still think it was okay to lie? e paced back and forth in front of the picture window. en she sat down, the old urge to take up a dare propel-g her to pick up her pen and a sheet of her new statio-ry.

She didn't say she had a forgiving nature or a desire to rt over. She just asked for details. He knew she'd answer ad. He knew she couldn't resist a dare. Then she sat back wait for his answer.

She wouldn't say she was anxious, but her days revolved ound her visit to the mailbox and her anxiety increased th each day that she didn't get an answer. She became ore nervous, jumpy and irritable as the weeks passed. No mber of guests could cheer her up, no telephone chats th Laurie, nothing.

One glorious winter day with the sun shining on the blue aters of the ocean below her house, she went down to the ach at low tide to try to get a new perspective on the sit-tion and to let the hypnotic crashing of the waves calm her rves.

Wearing shorts, a sweatshirt and canvas sneakers, she sat the wide, sandy beach and looked out beyond the reef to e horizon, until a large shape blocked her view and threw shadow across the sand. She rubbed her eyes with her nd.

"Adam." She dug her elbows into the sand to keep from ling over backward. He was wearing his same leather cket, the same intense expression in his dark eyes as the st time she'd seen him. Her heart pounded like a jack-mmer.

"I thought you might be down here," he remarked, si
ting down next to her as if he were some casual beac
comber instead of a geologist from the North Sea.

Mandy told herself to be calm. She told herself nothi
had changed but the weather since the last time they'd m
on this beach. But she couldn't stop her wildly beating hear
Couldn't stop hoping against hope that something else ha
changed, too.

"Did you get many answers to your ad?" she aske
looking into his dark eyes for a glimpse into his mind.

"Only one," he admitted. "So I thought I'd answer it
person."

She nodded, letting her gaze travel over his broad sho
ders and narrow hips, drinking in the sight of him like
woman stranded in the desert without water. "I thought
was you," she said. "But I was confused by the lonely m
lionaire part. The last time I saw you, you didn't plan to
lonely and you weren't a millionaire."

Adam moved as close to Mandy as he could witho
touching her, leaving only a half inch of sand between the
He turned his head to meet her inquiring gaze. Explaini
was not the hard part. Getting her to believe him was.

"I *was* a millionaire," he said. "I've always been or
since my dad died. He put the money for me into a tri
fund and I've never had reason to use it or tell anyone abo
it. It was just there."

"Then, why me? Why now?"

"I'm telling you now because I don't want to have a
more secrets from you. And because I might need some
the money. I just quit my job."

He heard her gasp, saw her tilt her head back and cl
her eyes. The sun picked up the sheen on her hair and l
hands itched with longing to run them through her s
curls, to pull her to him, to look deep into her eyes to fi

the answers to his questions. Did she believe him? Did she trust him? Did she want him?

"I was wrong about the drilling platform," he said soberly. "The thrills and the excitement, they couldn't compare to the thrills and excitement I found here with you."

She opened her eyes and looked at him. She wanted to believe, how much she wanted to believe. But if he didn't mean it, if he wasn't sure... She couldn't afford to take a chance. If he let her down again, it would kill her. "What if you'd had other answers to your ad?" she asked.

He shook his head. "There was only one person who fit the description, only one person I want for a long-term relationship."

"How long?" she asked, her eyelashes dark against her pink, windblown cheeks.

"Mandy," he said in a quiet voice. "I'm sorry about what happened. I was caught in a bind. I was supposed to be finding a wife for Jack, but when I saw you I wanted you all for myself. All those months, all those letters, and then there you were in person, better, more beautiful than I could have imagined. I wasn't only lying to you, I was lying to Jack. I told him you were an eight on a scale of ten."

Mandy jerked to a sitting position and turned her back on him. Her shoulders shook. She might have been laughing, she might have been crying, he couldn't tell. He just went on. He had no choice but to keep talking until she either walked away or told him she'd give him another chance.

"I even told him you might be a gold digger, I didn't know."

"Do you know now?" Her voice was muffled. He wanted to grab her by the shoulders and turn her around to face him and kiss her doubts away. But that wouldn't work. He had to talk them away or it was all over.

"Yes, I know. But you've got to know that I'm rich. And that I want to share my money with you. My life, too. Everything from now on."

She didn't speak.

"Oh, God, Mandy, would you say something, anything? Am I making any sense?"

She nodded. He saw her eyes were wide and luminous. Her lips, full and inviting. "Is that all?"

"There's more," he said, "but it will take hours, years, maybe, to unravel my personality. But you're acquainted with most of my faults by now."

"I guess I am, but I'm also acquainted with some of your assets, too. How kind you've been to me, how generous—not only to me but to your boss and to Jack."

He saw a dreamy smile curve at the corners of her mouth. He let himself hope for the first time that day.

"And that's not all," she continued. "You're sweet, scintillating and sexy, and I desire you very much. I have since the first day I saw you." She stared straight into his eyes with a passion that burned right through him.

He rubbed his chin and felt the heat rise up his neck. "You're embarrassing me," he mumbled, feeling his pulse accelerate. And that wasn't all she was doing to him.

She leaned over and brushed her lips across his. He blinked in disbelief. Did this mean what he thought it meant? He lay back on the sand and closed his eyes, letting her embarrass him as much as she wanted. He felt her palms against his, pinning him to the sand, then felt the heat of her mouth as she fit her lips against his and claimed him. Did this mean what he thought it meant, or was she just trying to shut him up?

She meshed her body against his, every hollow of his filled with every curve of hers. "One more thing, Mr. Lonely Millionaire," she said. "Just how long is long-term?"

"Forever," he said with a giant sigh of relief as he rolled over to give her a taste of forever right then and there on that deserted sunny beach a million miles from nowhere.

* * * * *

Get Ready to be Swept Away by
Silhouette's Spring Collection

Abduction
&
Seduction

These passion-filled stories explore both the dangerous
desires of men and the seductive powers of women.
Written by three of our most celebrated authors, they are
sure to capture your hearts.

Diana Palmer
Brings us a spin-off of her Long, Tall Texans series

Joan Johnston
Crafts a beguiling Western romance

Rebecca Brandewyne
New York Times bestselling author
makes a smashing contemporary debut

Available in March at your favorite retail outlet.

Take 4 bestselling love stories FREE

Plus get a FREE surprise gift!

Those Harris boys are back in book three of...

WEDDING WAGER

by Sandra Steffen

Three sexy, single brothers bet they'll never say "I do."
But the Harris boys are about to discover their vows of bachelor-
hood don't stand a chance against the forces of love!

You met Mitch in BACHELOR DADDY #1028 (8/94) and Kyle in
BACHELOR AT THE WEDDING #1045 (11/94). Now it's time for
brother Taylor to take the marriage plunge in—

EXPECTANT BACHELOR #1056 (1/95): When Gina Jenson sets
out to seduce the handsome Taylor, he's in for the surprise of his
life. Because Gina wants him to father her child!